HARRY THE POLIS
YE'RE NEVER GONNAE BELIEVE IT!

. . .

HARRY MORRIS

First published 2006
by Black & White Publishing Ltd
99 Giles Street, Edinburgh, EH6 6BZ

ISBN 13: 978 1 84502 121 4
ISBN 10: 1 84502 121 5

A CIP catalogue record for this book is available from the British Library.

Typeset by RefineCatch Ltd, Bungay, Suffolk
Printed by Nørhaven Paperback A/S

• • •

For Liz Kelly, a good friend

• • •

Acknowledgements

. . .

My sincere gratitude to all the loved ones, friends, family and acquaintances who stood by me and helped me along the long arduous road of expressing my love of the Glesca patter and my literary madness, which I shared with my colleagues and now with you in these pages.

You know who you are!

I want to express my love and appreciation to Marion for helping me realise my dream to forge a lifetime of stories and anecdotes into the writing of this book.

I'm also extremely grateful for the professional help and guidance I have been given by various newspapers and radio stations to accomplish my goal.

Thanks to John Downie and Bob Shields, who gave me valuable advice prior to the publication of the *Harry the Polis* books and have now become my good friends.

Special thanks to my friend Gordon Tourlamain.

Yours Aye,

Harry Morris

Slàinte!

'Ye just cannae beat Glesca for the real-life patter.'

The Old Age Alphabet

. . .

*This poem was given to my mother by a member of her church
and is a wee reminder of what happens to us all when old age
comes a-knocking.*

A is for ageing with its attendant delights.
B is for bladders, so active at nights.
C is for the cold, which I notice on waking.
D is for dinner, which I'll eat when not shaking.
E is for events, dreams stored in my head.
F is for future, a book still unread.
G is for ginseng, my pills full of mystery.
H is for hair, once lustrous, now history.
I is for inches, as I've aged, I've grown smaller.
J is for jiving, which I enjoyed when much taller.
K is for kidneys, causing problems for old fellows.
L is for lungs, my body's old bellows.
M is for memory, er . . . what was I discussing?
N is for name, once in my head but now missing.
O is for old but I've a rebellious streak.
P is for patronised, which I endure every week.
Q is for questioning, 'Am I adult or boy?'
R is for relatives, whose visits bring joy.
S is for siesta, naps to rest my old head.
T is for teeth, in a glass by the bed.
U is for uniform, my nursing carer's attire.
V is for volume, now required much higher.
W is for wrinkles, I still study with dismay.
X is for X-rays, revealing my inner decay.
Y is for my youth, now just a notion.
Z is for Zimmer, my means of slow motion.

Anon.

Sorry, Mam

• • •

It seems to me we all reach a certain age as a teenager and, not only do we know everything, but we become really cheeky and rude to our parents.

I'll submit a sample of my own smart talk, directed at my mother when I was about thirteen years old.

I entered the house, expecting it to be, as usual, occupied only with my sisters. Followed by two of my school friends, I thought I would show off and said in a loud voice, 'Where's the auld bag? I want something to eat!'

Unbeknown to me, my mother had come home early from work and walked out of a room behind me, coming between me and my pals and said, 'The auld bag is right behind you. Here, eat this!'

She then promptly took off her shoe and scudded me over the head with it!

Professional Mourner

• • •

This may sound unbelievable, but after you have retired from the police and you've caught up with a lot of the things that you dreamed of doing one day when you had more time, you suddenly and for no apparent reason begin to take an interest in the obituaries section of the police magazines.

Firstly to see who you know from the list of names of ex-cops that have unfortunately popped their clogs and secondly, and more importantly, to check your own name isn't on the list.

Then, totally out of the blue, I get an invite to a funeral from an ex-colleague – a bloody invite!

'Hi Harry, it's Donnie Henderson here! How's it hanging pal?'

And before I can answer, he nonchalantly slips it in: 'D'you fancy goin' along tae a funeral on Thursday? It'll be a right good yin. A big turn up is expected, without a vegetable in sight.'

He said it in the same way that you would expect him to ask, 'Hi Harry, d'you fancy going tae the ten pin bowling?' or 'D'you fancy going for a game of snooker and a few beers?'

'What are you all about, Donnie? Inviting me tae a funeral – huv ye been drinking or are ye just aff yer heid?' I replied angrily, before asking, 'Who is it that's getting buried anyway?'

There was a moment's pause, before he replied sarcastically, 'The deceased!'

'Well, I had already worked that out. So who was he?'

'Tam Spencer! Apparently he was the van driver at Hamilton,' he replied.

'What was the cause of death?' I asked, showing some concern for a fallen colleague.

'What?! All of a sudden you're fuckin' Quincy ME? How the fuck wid I know? I just read it in the paper but he died of something or they widnae be burying him!'

I thought for a moment then said, 'I don't think I know him.'

'Well, ye don't need to worry about it, Harry, 'cause ye're no' gonnae be introduced!' He paused for a moment before continuing, 'Look! There's gonnae be a big turn out at this, so we wear the funeral camouflage gear of black suit, white shirt and polis black tie, a wee poke in the eyes with yer finger to make them water and we're are in the funeral party mood.'

'You're a totally shameless and heartless man, Donnie,' I said, but my remark went right over his head.

'Listen tae this! The family are putting oan a free bar in the Black Bull after it. All relatives and friends – that's us – are invited to join them. You'll no' need tae spend a penny! Imagine it, a free bar!'

'D'you honestly think I would stoop that low for a free drink?' I said in utter disgust at this suggestion.

Donnie totally ignored my protestations and continued, 'And, wait for it, to help soak up the drink, a sit-down meal of home-made steak pie, totties and gravy!'

'A sit-down meal of steak pie, totties and gravy?' I repeated.

'And a free bar!' Donnie reminded me.

'So what time did you say we had to be there?'

'Good man, Harry boy. I'll pick you up at 11 a.m., so let's synchronise our watches,' he said excitedly. 'It'll be like a big party, without the host being present!'

Next day Donnie picked me up as arranged and off we went to Daldowie Cemetery.

When we arrived, there were already quite a few mourners waiting, so we mingled amongst them.

During the service, which went as well as a funeral service can, Donnie really got right into character for the part and at one point was sobbing uncontrollably. So much so that several people on either side of us handed him paper tissues.

As we left the cemetery and got into Donnie's car to follow the family to the Black Bull, Donnie said, 'What about my BAFTA performance in the church? Was I good or what?'

I was speechless, but I must admit, he was bloody good!

To crown it all off, the family had hired the services of an off-duty member of the police pipe band to play a lament at the graveside, which was a nice touch.

Unfortunately, being a typical pipe band member, he could drink like a fish and was even more inclined to do so since it was free.

When asked to play the funeral lament once more for the family members, he was that pissed he couldn't remember how it started, so he just played another old Scottish funeral favourite: *Will Ye No' Come Back Again*!

Not exactly his best choice for an off-the-cuff tune.

As a result, he was extremely lucky not to be wearing his bagpipes round his neck when asked to leave!

So, who knows, we might bump into each other at the next one.

First Class Examination

. . .

During a shift drinking session, one of the female officers was relating an unusual story about an incident when she had to undergo an examination with a gynaecologist.

Having showered and shampooed all her relevant bits and put on some nice new Marks & Spencer underwear, she made her way to the hospital for her appointment.

As she sat nervously in the waiting room, fidgeting away, the urge came over her to go to the toilet.

She got up from her seat and hurriedly made her way to the toilet. After she finished, she reached over for some toilet paper, but to her utter dismay, the holder was empty.

Panicking, she quickly searched through her handbag, frantically rummaging about the bottom for anything.

Fortunately, she found bits of old paper tissues and, using them to wipe her privates, she returned to the waiting room just in time to be summoned into the examination room by the nurse.

Once inside, she removed her clothing and put on a hospital gown, after which she was instructed to lie on the surgical table and place her legs in the stirrups, thereby spreading them.

Whilst lying there in this uncompromising position, the doctor moved in, wearing his miner's light on his forehead, to examine her.

Moments later, he removed something from her privates and looking up at the slightly embarrassed police woman, he handed her a 1st class postage stamp and said, 'I think this would look better attached to an envelope!'

The Prisoner of Harrogate

• • •

Young Alan Doran – nicknamed 'Supersonic' after the popular computer game character – and myself were performing plain-clothes duties when we received a call to return to the police office urgently.

On our return, we were instructed to take a CID car, drive to Harrogate Police Office in Yorkshire and escort a prisoner being detained there back to the Strathclyde area.

The reason for the urgency was to try and prevent us from incurring too many overtime hours. Therefore we were to drive straight down and back without any due delay.

Off we went on our journey and, after a few hours driving at maximum speed, we arrived at our destination.

I approached the front desk and identified myself to my English colleague, who was awaiting our arrival.

We were welcomed into the office area and informed that our prisoner was presently having his lunch and if we wanted to do likewise there were several good restaurants in the town centre nearby.

We took the advice of our colleague and made our way to the nearest cheap and cheerful McDonald's restaurant for a seventy-nine pence hamburger and a regular cup of coffee.

About an hour later, we returned to the police office to collect our prisoner.

'He's just coming, Jock! Won't be a minute,' said the male turnkey in his Yorkshire accent as he passed me by, carrying a dinner plate with some cutlery and a mug.

In his absence, I walked along the passage and looked into an open cell, where a prisoner was standing smoking a lit cigarette, which was sticking out from his mouth, and looking into a mirror on the wall while combing his hair.

He then glanced over at me standing in the doorway.

With one eye closed to avoid the smoke from his cigarette, he asked me, 'Are you here tae collect me for a trip back up the road, boss?'

'If your name's Donald Scullion, then I'm here for you!' I replied.

'That's me, boss, I'm yer man,' he answered. 'By the way, I would highly recommend this place tae get the jail. They're pure dead brilliant doon here and really friendly. No' like up the road!'

'What were you arrested for then?' I asked him.

'GBH!' he replied. 'I pure set aboot a young prick in the pub. He was trying tae noise me up in front o' his mates. So I introduced him tae a Glesca kiss, then glessed him wi' a pint tumbler. I made them aw pure shite themselves efter Ah done him!'

At that point, I reached over and removed the cigarette from his mouth and, throwing it to the ground, I stepped on it.

'Ye're not smoking in my car,' I said. 'And give me that comb as well,' I said as I grabbed it from his hand.

Just then the turnkey returned and Donny, the prisoner, said, 'See that, Georgie boy? That's how ye're supposed tae treat me 'cause I'm a ned or, as you say down here, a prisoner. Ye're aw pure dead brilliant guys, by the way, but ye're a bit too easy wi' yer prisoners, know whit a mean? Ye need tae harden up a bit and let them know who the boss is!'

I intervened, saying, 'Move it, big mouth!' and pushing him out into the cell passage, where Supersonic was waiting to fit him with some handcuffs.

As I collected his personal property from George, I followed Supersonic out the door to our CID car parked in the yard.

Donny, our prisoner, was placed in the rear of the car, accompanied by Supersonic, and I was just about to get into the front when George, the turnkey, came running out from the back door of the office waving a package.

'I forgot to give you Donny's cigarettes,' he said, handing them over to me.

'Aw thanks, George, ye're a pure gentleman!' shouted Donny from his seat in the rear of the police car.

As I drove out the yard, Donny said, 'Soon as I get oot, I'm coming right back here. The polis are jist pure brilliant. Ah could rule the roost doon here!'

'What made ye come down here in the first place?' asked Supersonic.

'Believe it or not, I wanted tae get aff the drugs and there's nae drugs doon here! Fuck me, even the chemist doesn't have a clue, I had tae pure educate him!'

'How come you educated the chemist?' enquired Supersonic.

Donny paused as he looked intently at Supersonic for a moment, then said, 'Know who you pure look like, wee man? That wee hedgehog computer cartoon guy.'

I interrupted Donny before he could finish: 'Don't even go there, just get on with yer story!'

'Right, okay, big man! Okay! Anyway, the first time I went in wi' my script tae the chemist for my methadone, he gave me the full week supply at once. I had tae tell him, "Hoy, chief, if you gie me that lot, I'll take hauf o' it mysel' in one go, then punt the rest tae another junkie."

'Then I told him, "You've got tae keep it here and gie me

my script once a day when I come in for it and I need tae take it in front o' you afore a leave the shop, 'cause I'm a pure junkie!'

'So ye're telling me you're an honest junkie then?' I asked him.

'Ah jist want tae get aff it boss and go clean!' he replied. 'By the way, ye could take this mob tae the cleaners doon here.'

'How come?' asked Supersonic, eager to learn.

'Easy! Ah had nae money when they lifted me, so they had a whip roun' amongst the officers in the station and raised twelve quid for me. They even bought me sixty fags oot their petty cash tae gie me a smoke. No' bad eh?'

'They gave ye money and cigarettes?' I repeated.

'Aye, and a different menu every night, tae pick yer grub. I've had a Chinky, a Chic Murray and, afore ye came tae collect me, I had some fuckin' fancy Italian pasta dish. It was pure dead brilliant, by the way!'

'How much money have you got in yer property?' I asked him.

'Twelve quid, Ah told ye. How come, boss?' he enquired.

'Because we only had a poxy hamburger while you were dining Italian like Al Pacino, so the first service station we come to with a McDonalds advertised, you're buying the grub!'

'No problem boss, but it will cost ye wan o' my snout,' he replied.

To which I responded, 'It's a meal deal, Donny boy, and I'll make mine large!'

Housewife's Menu

• • •

Once I had to attend a house in the Croftfoot area of Glasgow to check an arrested person's personal details and obtain confirmation that he resided at the address he had supplied to the arresting officers. I rang the bell and a female answered the door in her nightdress.

I thought to myself, 'That's a funny place to have a door.' (A wee bit of the old Chic Murray patter there!)

Anyway, she invited me into the house.

'Out of earshot of my nosy neighbours,' she explained.

Once inside her house, and having confirmed that the accused male was indeed her husband and resided there, I informed her that he had been arrested for a breach of the peace and would be detained in police custody until his appearance at court the following morning.

Instantly the female appeared to relax at this news regarding her husband's detention and said to me in a soft and suggestive voice, 'Can I interest you in some super sex?'

I completely misinterpreted her offer and replied in all sincerity, 'If it's alright with you, hen, I'll just settle for the soup!'

Thus confirming what everyone says about me that, if they cut a woman in half, I'd take the half that cooks!

Horses Up Closes
• • •

Two officers walked into the front office of the Castlemilk police station just as the bar officer was engaged in a heated telephone conversation.

'Look, ya bastart! If you phone here again, I'm going to trace this call and send the boys up tae yer door and jail ye, ya drug-swallyin' junkie. Now get a life!' He then slammed the telephone down on the desk.

'Whoa, Davie! That was a bit strong. What's yer problem?' enquired Dougie, concerned by Davie's obvious rise in stress levels, blood pressure and his big red baw face.

'This annoying druggie bastart, obviously oot his face, has telephoned me umpteen times tonight saying there's a big white horse up a close in Tormusk Road. I cannae even get making my tea in peace for him.'

He then paused for a moment before continuing with his rant. 'A fuckin' horse in Castlemilk! Don't make me laugh. If there was a horse in Castlemilk, there'd be a queue of fast food carry-out chefs chasing after it, along with several families!'

At that, he walked off along the corridor toward the kitchen to make his tea while muttering, 'Drugs! That's whit it is, drugs!'

As for Dougie and Jim, they left the office to continue with their police patrol of the area, totally convinced that Davie had lost his marbles and that inside running the station was probably the best place for him, rather than out roaming the range.

After a short time patrolling the area, Dougie just happened to check the rear-view mirror of the police panda. 'Ye're never going to believe this, Jim, but take a look behind us!'

As Jim turned around there, in full view, trotting up behind them was a young girl riding bareback on a big white horse.

Dougie pulled into the side of the road and they both got out of the car and signalled the rider to pull over with her horse.

'Where do you think you're going, Lady Godiva?' asked Dougie.

'I'm jist oot for a walk wi' my horse!' she replied confidently.

'Aye, right! Who does it belong to?' asked Jim, taking hold of the rope around its neck.

'Me! My Dah bought me it for my burfday!' she said.

'Birthday my arse!' interrupted Dougie. 'Where do you live?'

'The Mitchellhill Road flats!' she replied immediately.

'You live in the high flats? Who owns this horse? And don't dare lie,' Dougie warned her with a voice of authority.

'Ah don't know. I found it in a field near Carmunnock village.'

'I don't believe it! You just went into a field and helped yersel' tae somebody's pet horse and decided to ride it about the streets of Castlemilk! An area populated with more renegades than a John Wayne film! Are ye mad or what?' responded Jim.

They then helped the girl get off the horse and placed her in the rear of the police car, arresting her for the theft of the horse.

'Wait a wee minute!' said Dougie. 'Did you take this

horse up a tenement close in Tormusk Road earlier on tonight?'

'Aye! But I had tae – it wis raining and I didnae want it tae get wet! I tried to take it into the high flats, but it widnae fit into the lift,' the girl replied.

After some serious discussion, the two officers decided that Jim would lead the horse by the rope around its neck along the long road to the police office, closely followed by Dougie driving the police vehicle with the emergency blue roof lights fully illuminated and rotating.

The walk seemed to take an eternity for Jim, suffering the abusive and sarcastic remarks being shouted from the windows of the tenement houses along the route.

'Yer poliswomen are getting better looking!'

'Why the long face, big yin? Is that yer pack lunch?'

'Hey, Isa, check this horse wi' the big arse!'

But the best was: 'Yer burd's got a face like a horse. I'll bet she's a good ride!'

Finally, they arrived at the rear of the police office.

Now, tying the horse to the railings in the rear yard would have been far too easy, so they decided to wind up Davie, who was already totally demented by the numerous calls to the office regarding this big white horse seen up a tenement close.

So they led the horse in through the back door of the office, then shouted, 'Hey, Davie! Can you *Hopalong Cassidy* to the charge bar? We have a prisoner called Annie Oakley for you!'

'Nae bother!' was his reply, totally unaware of the surprise awaiting him!

'Yahoo!!'

A Hollywood Body Double

• • •

Whilst managing and performing in a Scottish folk band, I received a call one night from our roadie, Doogie.

'Hey, boss! I've just seen an advert for a guy who runs a video company in Edinburgh called Just-in View!' he said excitedly.

'And what about it, Doogie?' I asked him.

'Well, instead of having photographs taken of the band, why don't ye make a video of a live stage performance and send it out with all yer PR stuff tae organisers and promoters? Ye can even sell it at concerts.'

'They'll probably charge a fortune, Doogie, but give me the telephone number anyway,' I said in response, humouring him.

'When ye think about it boss, it's only two quid tae rent them out the video shop for three nights, so there ye go!' added Doogie.

'Aye right Doogie!' I replied, failing to see his point, but quickly acknowledging that the school days he missed through playing truant and plonking class as a boy were beginning to take their toll in his adulthood.

However, several days later, my curiosity got the better of me and I contacted the Just-in View video company to enquire about an estimated cost for making one.

'Hello, Just-in View video production company. Can I help you?' I was asked by some sissy on the other end of the phone.

'Oh, hello there. Is that Justin speaking?' I asked, in a deep macho voice.

'No, this is Jordan. I'm Justin's partner. On and off camera! What can I do for you?' he enquired of me in a rather softly-spoken, camp voice, which made me instantly respond by drawing the cheeks of my arse so tightly together you would have had a job sliding a cigarette paper between them!

'I'd like to price how much it would cost to make a live video of a six-piece Scottish folk band in concert action!' I said.

'A live show? Well let me see!' said Jordan. 'Six of you in tartan kilts! I take it you're all big, burly and randy then? No don't answer that, my mind is running away with itself.

'Right then! We will probably need to set up about five cameras just to get the best action shots and angles of you, so that'll involve more camera operators, but Justin will arrange that, he has another two pals with videos.

'Then there's the lighting! Justin will insist on having good lighting. So you'll have to check it out thoroughly for him.

'Another thing is make-up, darling! You will have to arrange your own make-up artistes. We just refuse to get involved with that side, too many prima donnas. And before you ask me, Justin does not have a "handsome" button on his video camera equipment, so whit ye see is whit ye get, sweetheart. It's a bloody camera he'll be using, no' a magic wand!

'You should see some of the sights we get asked to film. Especially weddings: talk about ugly brides! We've had them all.

'And fat! We are not talking pregnant here; I'm talking "Who ate all the pies?" fat! I think they were breast fed on Big Macs as weans! Fat hasn't a look-in. Justin had to fit a wide-angle lens to the camera, because of them.

'The brides were spreading over onto two and three frames.

'If they were models, they'd be on page 3 – and 4, 5 and 6, just to get their entire body in!

'So, in a nutshell, what I'm telling you is, if you have any uglies in the band, stick them at the back of the stage out of sight.'

I know immediately that my answer is going to be thanks but no thanks! However, I'm totally engrossed by this guy's lack of sales pitch, and I don't want to interrupt 'cause I'm loving his patter.

He continued in the same vein. 'Then, assuming we get all the film we require from the one live concert, and you'll be extremely lucky if we do, then Justin will set about editing it all together.

You'll probably want fade-in and fade-out sequences and we need to get the sound just right. I take it you have a sound engineer?' He asked, in his wee, soft, sissy-sounding voice.

'Yes!' I replied. 'We have our own sound engineer.'

'Good!'

'Venue?! What is the location of the venue? I presume you do have one, or am I being presumptuous?'

'Anyways, that's your problem, but if it is abroad I'll need to renew my passport, the bloody thing is expiring shortly – I'll also need to get a new photograph taken!'

'Enough!' I thought to myself, 'I need to intervene here.'

'So in a nutshell, Jordan, how much are we talking? Just give me a rough tally!'

'A rough tally?' he repeated. 'How about Al Capone? Now he was a rough tally. But if you mean can I give you a quote, then that's different!

'Right now! Let me think.' He then began muttering and mumbling over the phone, calculating it all for a price. Sorry, quote!

'About twenty-five to thirty thousand pounds, sweetheart! How does that suit you?'

'How does that suit me? Are ye aff yer fuckin' heid, sweetheart?' I responded instantly. 'For that kind of money, I'd be wanting Mel Gibson to play my part on stage!'

Return of the Mummy!
...

An old cop reluctantly took his wife and her ageing mother on a religious tour of the Holy Land.

Three days into the trip, his mother-in-law suddenly collapsed and died.

The old cop went off to see an undertaker about her body and was informed that at a cost of six thousand pounds he could arrange to have her body shipped back home to Scotland.

Alternatively, for the paltry sum of a hundred pounds he could arrange to have her buried in the Holy Land!

The old cop thought for a moment, then said, 'We'll just have her body shipped back home!'

'Are you sure about that?' asked the undertaker. 'There's an awful big difference in the costs.'

'Yeah I know,' said the old cop, 'but about two thousand years ago, they buried a guy here and three days later he rose from the dead! I'm just not prepared to take any chances with the auld yin!'

Lessons in Elocution

• • •

As a young man I was considered a very good footballer. In fact, to tell you the truth, I was bloody brilliant!!

My skills were in such demand I had more trials than Donald Finlay! And played with more clubs than Jack Niklaus!

However, enough of my modesty.

Due to my prowess on the football park, I naturally played for my police divisional team. One particular day, big Alex Smith, the pay clerk within the police who doubled up as the football team manager, approached me.

'You're playing football today, Harry!' he said.

'Naw am urnae!' I replied rather bluntly.

He looked at me rather puzzled, before repeating, '"Naw am urnae?" What language do you speak, son? I take it you meant to say, "No I am not"!'

'Well! Naw aye am not!' I replied condescendingly.

To which Alex responded facetiously, 'Aye ye ur!'

I then looked at him for a moment, before replying sarcastically, '"Aye ye ur"? I take it you meant to say, "Yes you are"?'

'Naw!' he replied rather indignantly. 'I mean ye bloody ur sought, or else!'

Munchtime Menu

. . .

Out on traffic patrol over in the west end with my new partner Tom Jack, we were heading along Dumbarton Road, making our way back to the traffic department for our lunch break when Tom enquired if I had a pack lunch with me, or was I having to buy something?

I informed him I was just going to get a salad roll from the local baker's shop, next to the traffic office.

'Don't bother,' said Tom. 'My sister and brother-in-law own a chip shop just along the road. We can stop off and get a lunchtime special or a bag o' chips.'

Never having been one to refuse a free meal, I readily agreed.

After we had travelled a short distance Tom said, 'This is it on the left here.'

As I pulled up outside the front door the shop lights were on. We both got out of the police car and went over to the door, but soon discovered the front door was locked.

'That's funny!' remarked Tom. 'They're usually always open for the lunchtime special.'

Tom then knocked several times on the glass door, but there was no reply.

'They're maybe not opening today!' I said, making an excuse for him.

'No, they must be! The lights are on. They must be in the back shop and can't hear us,' he said. 'Let's go around the back and take a look!'

At that, I followed Tom through the close mouth to the backcourts and we approached the back door, which was also locked.

'The lights are on,' I said, as I stood on a box and leaned

over to look through the window. And there in the back shop, on a table beside the filleted haddock fish and chipped potatoes, participating in some erotic oral sex, were a male and a female.

As I stepped back down, I said to Tom in my own imitable style, so as not to embarrass him, 'I know why yer brother-in-law and his missus weren't answering the door. She's got her mouth full and he has his hands full!'

Tom looked over at me, puzzled, and replied, 'What? Let me see,' as he brushed me aside, eager to get to the window for a bird's eye view.

Stepping onto the box, he leaned over and looked through the window, where he observed her obvious expertise for several moments like a professional voyeur before losing his balance and slipping off the box.

'Thank goodness for that,' I said. 'I was beginning to think you were a bit of a pervert, eye-balling yer brother-in-law and yer sister at it.'

Tom looked at me totally stunned and speechless. He was gobsmacked by what he had just witnessed.

'Don't worry about it, Tom, I won't say anything. After all, they are yer family. And they both looked like they were enjoying their lunchtime special!'

Tom interrupted me. 'That's not what's worrying me. It's the fact that she's my wee sister, but he's definitely not my brother-in-law! Seriously, Harry! What do you think I should do about this?' he asked in a concerned way, seeking my mature, professional and logical advice.

I paused for a moment while considering my reply, then I said dismissively, 'Simple! Just forget about the chips, Tom, and buy a salad roll from the baker's like me!'

Battle of the Boyne

· · ·

The Strathclyde Police Force control room is based at police headquarters in Glasgow.

It generally receives all 999 emergency calls and controls all the police vehicles in the area. It is run by police personnel performing the work of the telephone operators/controllers and the entire operation is overseen by a duty officer, normally of inspector rank.

Back in the 80s, one such inspector was Willie Whitelaw, one of life's real gentlemen. Nothing ever got to him or got him excited and he was extremely laid back. So laid back, as they say, that he was horizontal.

Trouble had been brewing between rival gangs in the Drumchapel area over a period of several weeks and one Friday evening things came to a head when the two gangs met to do battle on some spare ground.

It would have been like a scene out of *Braveheart*. They were armed with baseball bats, knives and even samurai swords.

Suddenly all the red telephone 999 lights lit up in the police control room from the anxious residents keen to report the carnage going on.

All available cars were directed to attend the location.

Constable Stewart Boyne, one of the radio controllers, assumed charge of the situation and hastily arranged for patrol cars from other divisional areas to attend as well.

He was also hearing things from officers at the scene.

'More assistance is required urgently!'

Stewart responded in a reassuring manner, 'Station calling, please note the support unit are attending and will be with you very shortly.'

Back came the abrupt reply, 'THIS IS THE SUPPORT UNIT!!'

Things were going from bad to worse and Stewart was having to look further afield for assistance and was soon arranging for cars to attend from the south side of the city via the Clyde Tunnel.

He was sweating buckets, as they say, and it was becoming very stressful to deal with, even though he was in the relative safety of the force control room.

Willie Whitelaw, the duty officer, was sitting back in his chair and was pleasantly impressed by the efforts of his young controller, managing to cope, to a certain extent, with the incident, through all the noise and distractions of the control room.

Suddenly Willie shouted over to him, 'Stewart!'

Stewart looked up from his control console and replied, 'Yes, Inspector!'

Willie then asked, 'Can you get me an exact grid reference for that location?'

Stewart was all flustered and couldn't understand why he should ask for such a thing at such a hectic time and therefore nervously replied, 'What? Now, sir?'

'Yes, now!' replied Inspector Whitelaw, before continuing, 'I'm going to contact the RAF to see if they can organise an air strike on these bastards!'

Everyone in the control room at first looked at him in disbelief, then burst into fits of laughter.

It was a great tonic and helped calm everyone down sufficiently to deal with the incident.

In the meantime, the cops at the location were still dealing with a serious running battle and were probably quite bemused to hear their radio controllers sniggering over the airwaves!

Piss Artist

. . .

Along with my colleague Colin Muir, or, should I say, 'Gallus', as he was better known by the neds in the area, we attended a complaint of a disturbance within the high rise flats at Shawbridge Street, in Pollokshaws, Glasgow.

We entered the foyer and pressed the button for the elevator.

A few moments later, while standing in front of the entrance to the door, the elevator arrived and opened.

As we made to enter we were stopped in our tracks by the sight of a drunken women in her mid-forties, squatting down in true Carol Thatcher fashion in one corner of the elevator, dressed head-to-toe in a thick fur coat and resembling Hercules the bear, her knickers dangling around her ankles, pissing.

It's amazing how much urine a coat made from an animal's fur can soak up, but it managed every last drop! It was probably the cleanest elevator floor in the entire area, after we left.

And therein lies an interesting debate.

What's the best waterproof: synthetic or real fur?

Strictly Dancing

· · ·

One evening, I took my latest girlfriend up to my parent's house in Pollok.

Only my father was in the house, so I introduced her to him.

'Dad, this is Mary. Mary, this is my dad, Fred. Now you two chat between yourself, while I go upstairs and get changed. We're going out dancing!'

At that, I went upstairs to get ready.

Whilst I was upstairs and out of earshot, my father asked Mary, 'So Mary! Do you screw?'

'I beg your pardon, Mr Morris?' replied Mary, taking exception to his question.

This just prompted my father to repeat his question, 'I asked, do you screw?'

At that point, Mary jumped up from her seat, grabbed her coat and ran from the house.

Moments later I returned to the front room where Mary had been chatting with my father.

'Where's Mary?' I asked my dad.

'She just got up out of her seat and left the house!' he replied.

I threw myself down onto the sofa seat beside him.

'Right, dad, what did you say to her?' I asked him dejectedly.

'I didn't say anything, son!' he replied in all innocence.

'You must have said something to upset her and cause her to run from the house. Now what did you say?' I asked again.

He shook his head, then replied rather sheepishly, 'I just asked her if she screwed.'

Exasperated by this remark, I said, 'How many times must I tell you, dad? It's, "Do you TWIST?"'

That's My Brother

· · ·

I was invited to a New Year party at a police colleague's house, during which he put on a cassette of music for me to listen too.

'Wait till you hear this, Harry! It's my brother Frankie singing and playing all the percussion!' he said proudly.

I listened for a few tracks and the voice became so very distinct, very professional and very, very familiar that, not wanting to embarrass him, I said, 'I'm sure I've heard him before, I definitely recognise the voice!'

However, one of our female police colleagues overheard me talking and interrupted, assuredly saying to me, 'Of course you recognise the voice, it's bloody Joe Longthorne. I've got that very same cassette in the house. He even impersonates Shirley Bassey singing *Big Spender* on it!'

Then turning to John she said sarcastically, 'Now, I don't suppose yer brother does that, John! Or does he?'

Poor old John, the proud, gullible brother – he didn't know where to look!

Sex and Marriage

· · ·

One day while sitting having my refreshment break with a young probationer cop, we were discussing sex and marriage.

'I never even slept with my wife before I married her. What about you, Harry?' he asked me.

I thought for a moment, then said, 'I'm not really sure, son! What was her maiden name?'

Stuck for an Answer

. . .

While working on a major incident, logging all the productions involved, I received a call to come and see the new acting chief inspector, who brushed into the office like a new broom!

I knocked on his door and was beckoned in and invited to take a seat opposite him, before he put the question to me, 'Can you please tell me why you are not wearing your uniform?'

As I sat across from him, dressed in my T-shirt and denim jeans, I decided to just bluff it and said with total conviction, 'Tell you the truth, boss. I just couldn't be bothered wearing it!'

He sat with a vacant look trying to digest what I had just said and desperately seeking a response to my frank and shameless reply.

'You what? You just couldn't be bothered wearing it? Get out! Go on, get right out!' he replied, displaying his irate character.

However, later the same day I was summoned back to his office and informed that he had just transferred me to the courts branch, so I had 'better be bothered' and put on my uniform, pronto!

Ach! The young gaffers of today: they just cannae take a joke!

Cowboy Snips

· · ·

From *The Adventures of Harry the Polis*

(Harry and Spook are in the front of the police office.)

HARRY: What were you off sick with, Spook?
SPOOK: I was in de 'ospital getting me a vasectomy.
HARRY: I knew it – you were in for the old snip!
SPOOK: Dat's right man, I got me da old snip!
HARRY: Let me guess! You were in the Western Infirmary.
SPOOK: Now how did ya know dat, man?
HARRY: Because all morning you've been walking around
      like big John Wayne, minus his horse!

(Next day at the office.)

HARRY: Hey, Spooky boy. Did you see the news last night?
SPOOK: Why?! What about dit man?
HARRY: That doctor who performed your snip – he's
      been struck off and doesn't practice medicine
      any more.
SPOOK: How come dat then?
HARRY: Apparently, while performing another vasectomy
      he let his scalpel slip and got the sack!

Marathon Man

• • •

During the mid-eighties, while a member of the motor-cycle section, I had the honour of being the lead, with a 'Follow me' sign on the rear of my bike, for the runners competing in local marathons.

It was also a great money-earner for close friends at my local public house, when they would willingly and confidently give out very good odds and accept bets from anyone present as to who would cross the winning line first with a few miles to go in a long gruelling race.

'I'll put a fiver on Charlie Spedding crossing the line first; no one is going to catch him now!'

Another punter would add, 'Yeah! I'll have some of that. Put me down for a tenner!'

All bets would be readily accepted by my mates, then all eyes would be on the finishing line as the many TV cameras focused on the leading contenders, the punters confident of winning their bet as Charlie Spedding, the leading athlete was ahead by a mile.

A loud cheer would go up from the punters as the lead runner neared the finish, only for a louder cheer to go up from my mates as I crossed the finish line first.

'Yes! First over the finish line is Harry Morris!' one of my excited mates, performing the role of bookie for the day, announced to the entire pub gathering.

'It was Charlie Spedding who won the race!' argued a punter.

'Yes he did, mate, but the bet was the first to cross the finish line and that was Harry Morris!' replied my mate.

Unconvinced by this decision the punter then asked the bookie, 'Who the fuck was Harry Morris and where was he in the race?'

My mate would then confidently inform him, 'Harry Morris, my friend, was the big polis on the motorbike who crossed the finish line first!'

This decision was not exactly popular with strangers to the pub.

As a result of this particular duty I collected six Glasgow Marathon medals, one Kirkintilloch Half Marathon medal and a Clydebank Half Marathon medal.

However, it was during the short Clydebank Half Marathon that disaster almost struck.

As usual, prior to the day of the event, I attended Clydebank Police Office for a briefing about the race.

Afterwards, I was taken outside, where I followed the Divisional Chief Inspector on my motorbike as he was driven round the route to be followed.

Due to the many pedestrian shoppers within the Clydebank Shopping Centre we were unable to go over the final few hundred metres but I was assured by the chief inspector that the event would be well lined with many volunteer stewards on the day.

Come the day of the race, I duly arrived at the start of the half marathon event in plenty of time and went over the route, checking there were no obvious or unexpected obstructions that might cause me a problem once the race event got under way.

As I entered the shopping centre, I was met with a posse of yellow jacket-clad stewards, all congregated to receive their instructions from the race organisers.

Noting they were all busily being made aware of their duties, I headed back to the main area, where the participating athletes were gathered anticipating the start of the race.

A short time later we were off, and the more professional athletes amongst the many participants soon set the pace for the serious contenders.

Several miles later, a gap was appearing between the first runner and the rest.

A spectator lining the route, obviously recognising the leading athlete as a local lad, called out, 'C'mon, Nat! You can dae it, son. Just imagine that big polis on the motorbike is at yer back trying tae catch ye!'

With less than a mile to go to the finish, we entered the shopping centre, which I anticipated would be congested with spectators wanting to view the winner on his way to the finishing line, and brimming with race stewards directing the way.

To my complete horror, there was no one in sight, so much so, I had to stop and look around to see if I could spot a steward, or indeed anyone, to provide me with directions, but nobody was in attendance.

By this time, the leading runner had caught up with me and was now running on the spot, frantically asking me, 'Where are we going? Where's the finish line?'

I had no answer and was beginning to panic myself, as I saw two other runners appear in the near distance, a few hundred metres behind.

Having also noticed the other runners closing in on him, the lead runner began shouting at me, whilst running in circles around my motorcycle, 'Come tae fuck, big man! Which way is it now?'

I was just about to tell him I hadn't the foggiest idea, having never been shown the finishing line, when a yellow-vested steward staggered out from a nearby public house and directing me with a half empty pint glass in his hand shouted, 'Ho, big man! Up there and ye better run like the clappers, 'cause they're nearly up yer jacksy oan the telly!'

With those kind words of coaching advice given, I quickly proceeded in the direction in which he had pointed.

Fifty metres along the road, we saw the finish line and, boy, was I ever glad to see it, as was the leading runner.

I slowed down just enough to allow the lead runner to race on by me to the finish tape, closely followed by the chasing pack, who, during our unplanned time-out break for directions, had closed the gap considerably.

This was one victorious winner who was not en-amoured of his police escort, the race organisers or their voluntary stewards.

Use of Words
...

The superintendent called me into his office one day and said, 'I've called you in, Morris, to discuss two words in your vocabulary that you use regularly when involved in discussions. One is "brilliant" and the other, is "minging"!'

'Okay, sir!' I said. 'What are they then?'

Sharing My Swearing

· · ·

When I was a very young boy, I had a terrible speech impediment.

Well it wasn't so much a speech impediment, it was more that I tended to swear like a trooper, as they say, and I was regularly battered by my father for doing so.

It was a few weeks before Christmas and my mother warned me that if I didn't stop swearing Santa Claus would not bring me any presents.

I struggled with my impediment, desperate to stop swearing, and, before I knew it, it was Christmas Eve.

After lunch I started an argument with my sisters, where I called them names peppered with some colourful swear-words.

This was the final straw for my mother and she grabbed me and put me into my room to get ready for bed early with the threat that she was going to tell my father about my behaviour when he arrived home from his work.

A short time later I had fallen asleep and, when my father arrived home from his work, my mother duly informed him about my continued cursing.

He decided it was time to teach me a lesson, once and for all, in an attempt to cure my bad language.

On Christmas Day, the following morning, I awoke early to find a metal bucket filled to the brim with steaming horse manure sitting on the floor at the bottom of my bed.

I looked around the rest of my room, but there were no presents littering the floor, just this smelly bucket of fresh horse manure.

I picked it up by the handle and wandered into my sisters' bedroom.

'Hi, Linda! What did you get from Santa?' I asked her.

'I got a doll, a pram, a new coat and a chocolate selection box,' she said, absolutely delighted with her gifts.

I then turned my attention to my other sister, Kim, and asked her, 'And what did you get, Kim?'

'Oh, I got a desk and chair, a blackboard and chalk, a new dress and a big box of jelly babies!'

As I stood there holding onto my bucket, brimming with steaming horse manure and looking on enviously at the girly presents they had been given by Santa, my sister Linda asked, 'And what did you get from Santa, Harry?'

To which I replied, 'I got a horse, but I'm fucked if I can find it!!'

Acupuncture
· · ·

My mother was describing the fact that my brother-in-law, Archie, had undergone a course of acupuncture to help him lose weight. It involved pins with round ends being placed at pressure points.

She said, 'So whenever he feels hungry, he rubs his balls behind his ears.'

Which makes me think he went to a yoga class by mistake! Either way, if it's true he should definitely include it in a circus act!

She'll Give You One

· · ·

It is amazing how we can have other people working in our midst and we don't for a second give any thought to what their interests outside the job might be.

Such was the case with an elderly woman traffic warden who worked out of a certain police office in South Lanarkshire. Rutherglen, to be precise!

She never displayed a great deal of personality around the office and, indeed, I would say she was quite an unassuming wee woman, who went about totally unnoticed and with the minimum of fuss. She would never warrant a second look from any members of the opposite sex.

To be really brutal, she was a wee, dumpy, grey-haired granny!

However, her profile was about to rise rapidly when, one day, the uniformed station officer somehow, and I've never figured this one out yet, just happened to be perusing a pornographic magazine during his refreshment break. As one does, I'm told!

Whilst sitting there, in the toilet, I presume, reading away and viewing the colourful pictures, he turned to the page referred to as 'Readers' Wives' and there, posing in various uncompromising positions, like a haddie (she smelt of fish), and wearing nothing but an old pair of black suspenders and a false-teeth smile courtesy of the NHS, was our very own voluptuous wee, dumpy, grey-haired traffic warden, Senga. Or, as the magazine article referred to her, 'Sexy Seductive Senga Sluts Her Stuff'.

Apparently, she had undergone a breast enlargement operation prior to her explicit photographic session and had gone from a 32A to an impressive 34DD (Droopy Diddies).

However, she needn't have bothered, for her breasts were sagging that low, they resembled an Ikea flat pack! Allegedly!

It appears that during her time as a traffic warden she was handing out more than just her parking tickets to drivers! What a nice surprise for a driver running out from the newsagent's to discover that the traffic warden didn't put a parking ticket under his windscreen wiper but left her colourful card!

Even more amazing was how popular she became around the office after news of her explicit naked pictures in the magazine coupled with the descriptions of her sexual exploits were made public!

Ministry of Laughs
. . .

Kevin Flett was the local minister of the Baptist church in Cambuslang and the congregation of his ministry were genuinely delighted and excited when he announced his wife had given birth to not one baby girl but two.

Yes, twin girls!

'What are you going to name them?' asked several of the older female church members.

To which Kevin, the proud father, replied with a straight face and his wonderful dry wit, 'Lea and Pam!'

Several Sunday services passed before the penny dropped with them all that the children would be referred to as 'Lea Flett' and 'Pam Flett'!

Kevin was also well known for his paper handouts in church.

Chivas Down My Spine

...

Whilst still in my police probation period and working my first Christmas day public holiday alongside 'Soapy', the carbolic alcoholic, on the divisional Land Rover, we received a call from some concerned neighbours who reported an elderly male failing to answer his door.

We attended the address and, after forcing the main door to gain entry, our worse fears, and that of his neighbours, were realised as we discovered the elderly male sitting propped up in his bed and stiff as a board.

Having just got into bed on Christmas Eve he had suffered a massive heart attack, which had proved fatal.

After dealing with the neighbours and noting the relevant details required for our sudden death report, Soapy and I were left alone in the house to await the arrival of the undertakers.

As we were looking around the house for other relevant information, with regards to relatives, etc, I couldn't help but notice there was a bottle of Chivas Regal Whisky most notably present on the bedroom dresser beside the deceased's bed and a glass of whisky sitting on the bedside table. Obviously his nightcap!

Soapy became very agitated and began fidgeting about and bending down to look at the level of the whisky in the bottle, focussing with one eye closed on the whisky in the glass.

He then opened the whisky bottle and, lifting the glass, carefully poured it back into the bottle without spilling a drop.

Having performed this task, he bent down again, closing one eye to look at the level, before saying with excitement in his voice, 'Ah knew it! The auld bugger had just opened that brand new bottle and poured himself a hauf afore he croaked. He never even touched it!'

I stood for moment puzzled as to his reaction and wondering what I had missed. I just had to ask, 'So what? He didn't drink it. What's your point?'

'Exactly, Harry my boy, he didn't!' At that, he poured the whisky into the glass again and raising it up to toast the deceased male, he promptly drank it down!

This, I suppose, was his way of showing me my first taste of Christmas spirit within the police.

I still get Chivas down my back when I think about it!

Can't Wait to Tell Her

· · ·

I was visiting a colleague at his house while he was off sick and I was saying that I had just recovered from a heavy cold.

'Heavy cold!' said his wife. 'I've just got over the flu.'

'My wife had a bad bout of the flu!' I said, making conversation.

'Flu!' she said. 'I was that bad, it went into pneumonia. It took me weeks to get over it. Anyway, I'll away and make the tea and leave you two to talk!' At that, she left the room.

As I turned to my ailing colleague, he said dejectedly, 'You'll notice If you have the cold, she has the flu. If you have the flu, she has pneumonia. If you have a rash, she has eczema!

'I can't wait to hear what she has when I tell her I have cancer!'

Whit's In The Bag?

• • •

At Tulliallan Police College we were given a lecture by the wee local guy that teaches the first aid course. He was describing a scenario of an incident that occurred in the Fife area and said, 'This man, this diabetic self-injecting man – and there lies the first clue to his death – was found one particular morning lying stone dead in a farmer's field.

'Several metres away from where he lay was a bag containing the thing that could and would have saved his life. Suffice to say, if he had opened the bag earlier, he would still be alive!

'What exactly would he have needed to carry in his bag?'

I couldn't resist the temptation and shouted out, 'A parachute!'

Much to the hysterical amusement of my fellow students!

Musical Porn in Maryhill

• • •

Driving past a secondary school in the Maryhill area of Glasgow, I noticed they were advertising a school musical being performed by the pupils.

The musical was,
'SEVEN BRIDES FOR SEVEN BROTHERS!'

Later the same day, I had occasion to pass it again and as I looked over, I couldn't help but burst out laughing, as some local wag had rubbed out a letter in order for it now to advertise, **'SEVEN RIDES FOR SEVEN BROTHERS!'**

The Remote Remote

· · ·

Visiting my elderly parents' house one day, I was treated to view the brand new, remote-controlled, twenty-eight inch coloured television.

'Watch this!' my dad proudly said. 'Right, Flora.'

My mother got up from her seat, went over to it and, lifting the remote control from the top of the television, she stood in front of it and began to change the station.

'What about that then, son? Fully remote-controlled Nicam TV and teletext: now that's progress. Although I don't know what the hell this teletext is, or how ye get it,' he said, before continuing, 'Right, sit down out the road, Flora, we cannae see it for you!'

At that, my mother replaced the remote control neatly on top of the TV and sat back down beside my father to view it.

'That's no' whit we were watching, Flora. Put it back onto the channel we were watching,' he said. 'I was enjoying that other programme.'

'Oh right.' She struggled up from her seat, walked over, picked up the remote control, stood in front of the TV and flicked through the channels, before replacing it neatly back on top of the TV and returning to her seat.

'Wait a minute, mam!' I said. 'You don't have to get up and down to change a channel station, ye just have your remote control beside you, point it at the TV and press the channel you want. That's the whole idea about having a remote control – it's to save you from having to get up and down.'

I took the remote control from the top of the TV and, sitting back down on my seat, I demonstrated changing the station and adjusting the volume control.

When I stopped, I placed the remote control on the arm of the chair where I was sitting.

My parents remained seated watching me do this, until my mother, expressing herself rather indignantly, said, 'Oh no ye don't, son! Just put that back on top of the TV. That way it doesn't get lost and we always know exactly where it is for changing the stations!'

Trying to argue the point was not an option with my mother when she had made up her mind.

For several months they operated it in this way, with my mother getting up from her seat to use the remote control on top of the TV to change a station, before she eventually got fed up and decided to keep it at the side of my father's armchair.

Now that was progress!

Him and Her
. . .

On a night out to the Pavillion Theatre I was about to enter the main door, when I was stopped by a foreign visitor to Scotland who wanted to know what to ask for when he entered the theatre.

'Simple! I said. 'Just follow me and do as I do.'

With that said, I entered the theatre and went up to the box office and said, 'Two tickets for *Francie and Josie* please!'

After I had paid and received my tickets, I stood back and beckoned the foreign visitor to step forward and do likewise. He then stepped forward and asked the box office assistant for, 'Two tickets for Ivan and Olga!'

Post Office Pete

· · ·

'Post Office Pete' is an old fellow with a dry sense of humour whom I've seen several times when sending off my parcels from the local post office.

He's about 5' 6" in height, with hunched shoulders, grey hair covered with a wee bunnet, thick spectacles and a hearing aid, but the most distinctive thing about him is that he wears a jacket decorated with his war medals and has a badge on his breast pocket which reads, 'Normandy Veteran 1944'.

The other day, I walked into the post office to send off some mail and there was PO Pete, as usual, standing in the queue.

There was another elderly man several places in front of him, who looked behind at the line and recognised Pete.

'Oh hi there, Pete!' he said.

'Hello, Tam!' he replied.

'Did ye hear auld Ella had an operation on her eyes?' he asked.

'Yes, I know!' replied Pete.

'Oh, ye know. Did you hear how she got on then?'

'Aye! Apparently the operation was a huge success,' said Pete. 'Unfortunately for her!' he added.

Tam was puzzled by this reply. 'Why do ye say unfortunately, Pete?'

'Well it was bad enough for her when she had to suffer listening to Bob all day, but now she'll be able to see him as well.'

Tam thought for a moment, then said, 'Aye! Right enough, Pete, I never thought about that!'

Tam then moved up the queue, before turning back

towards Pete and looking at his Normandy veteran badge. He said, 'I had my old squadron leader over yesterday!'

Quick as a flash Pete responded, 'Don't tell me! It was a flying visit, so he just dropped in!'

'Naw! Naw!' replied Tam. 'We had arranged a game of golf.'

'A squadron leader that can play golf, that's amazing!' responded Pete in a condescending voice.

'He got off to a flyer and birdied the first two holes,' said Tam.

Pete shook his head. 'Amazing! You make me wish that I had joined the RAF!'

Tam moved forward again in the line before turning back to Pete, who asked, 'Have you seen that David Blunkett's new girlfriend?'

Tam replied in all innocence, 'Naw! I have not!'

To which Pete took great satisfaction in saying, 'Well don't worry about it, 'cause neither has he!'

Unknown to Me

· · ·

I regard myself as PC Illiterate and I say that because, one day, I was working at a busy main street when I was approached by a young couple and asked if I knew the whereabouts of PC World.

Assuming they were referring to a police colleague, I promptly answered, 'I have no idea – I don't even know if he is working today!'

Control Room Patter

· · ·

An emergency 999 call was received at the force control room, where a lady was complaining that she had just looked out of her bedroom window and there was a young couple fornicating on the bonnet of her car!

The woman caller decided to remain on the telephone and give to the operator a blow-by-blow account of everything they were doing in great detail and much more explicitly than was required.

Much to the delight and excitement of the radio operator, I might add. It saved him money on the chat line!

However, assault with a friendly weapon is not exactly a serious crime that requires blue lights and blaring sirens, so the operator prepared an incident report on his PC and sent it to the local police office serving the area to deal with it.

It was a very odd complaint to receive so before going off duty the original operator decided to check the result of the complaint and whether any police action had been taken.

This is a copy of the original result, supplied by the officer who attended.

Inspector Duffy, he attended the call,
But there was no one there at all.
The couple, allegedly making love on the
bonnet,
Had come then gone and definitely had
done it!
And that's the final result of the call.

Boom! Boom!

Mickey's Pal

• • •

After a short chase, I apprehended a young male mugger who had ripped a handbag from an elderly woman. I then summoned the police van and conveyed him to Craigie Street police office.

As I stood with him waiting at the charge bar, the officer on duty came through to note the charge and the personal details of the accused male.

The detention charge blotter, in the shape of a large black book, was produced and opened by the OD Inspector Willie Hamilton.

'Right, what's the charge?' asked the inspector.

I read out the charge, which he noted in the charge blotter, and after I was finished Inspector Hamilton directed his attention toward the young accused male, disgusted with his actions towards a frail, defenceless and elderly woman.

'Right you, what's yer name?' he asked in disgust.

The accused looked at him and said, 'Are you talking tae me, big man?'

'Well I know the name of the police officer holding you, so I would reckon it's a safe bet I'm talking to you! Now what's yer name?'

The accused male stared at the officer on duty for a moment, before replying, 'Walt fuckin' Disney!'

The OD looked at him and said, 'Don't mess with me, son! I'm no' in the mood. Now what's your name?'

'Okay!' replied the ned. 'It's Donald!'

'Donald what?' enquired the OD writing in the charge book.

'Naw! No' Donald Watt, pal – Donald Duck, as in Mickey's pal!' he replied, sniggering at the same time.

The OD looked straight at him, before noting his 'name' into the detention book.

'And where do you stay, Mr Duck?' asked the OD, smiling.

The accused continued sniggering and laughing nervously as he replied, 'Queen's Park fish pond.'

All the time, my colleague and I stood holding an arm each, trying desperately not to join in the laughter.

Meantime, the OD smiled openly, closed the large black detention blotter, raised it above his head, and brought it crashing down on the head of the accused – a 'BLOOTER'! Not 'blotter'!

The legs of the accused buckled under him.

'Hold him up,' ordered the OD, who had lost his patience.

As we did so, the large blotter came crashing down on top of his head again – Wallop!!

As the smile rapidly disappeared from the face of the now totally dazed ned, the OD said, 'Well, Mr Duck! Guess what?

'Donald gets the jail, but Walt fuckin' Disney!'

Go on then!
· · ·

One morning, my missus and I were enjoying a cup of coffee in bed together, when our pet Yorkie, Jock, jumped up onto the bed, causing her to almost spill hers.

My missus, only just avoiding an accident, shouted out, 'No, Jock! Absolutely no way are you getting into my bed.'

Just at that point, our friendly postman was walking past our open window and on hearing this outburst, he shouted back, 'Oh let him in, ya temptress!'

Andy and the Hot Cross Buns

· · ·

There was a knock at the rear door of the office and, when I opened it, in came the relief sergeant of the following shift, carrying a plastic bag with two hot cross buns in it.

'You're early, Jack!' I said, as I opened the door to him.

'I've got court at two o'clock, so I stopped off at the wee baker's shop in Lanark and bought myself a couple of hot cross buns. They're the best.' As he placed them on the kitchen table, he said, 'Be back in a minute, Harry, I'm just popping out for a jar of coffee!'

Moments later, there was another knock at the rear door. This time it was big Andy Murphy, the police van driver, calling in for a quick cup of tea.

'You don't mind if I have a quick cuppa, Harry?' he asked.

'Not at all, Andy, help yourself,' I said obligingly.

Minutes later Andy shouted through, 'These hot cross buns are crying out to be eaten!'

So I shouted back, 'Well you better not, let them down!'

Andy accepted this as an invitation to eat them and quickly devoured them both in no time at all, before bidding me farewell and leaving by the rear door.

As in all good pantomimes, as one door closes another door opens.

In this case, the bad guy (big greedy Andy) had left by the rear door, as the good guy (the hungry sergeant) returned by the front!

Armed with his jar of coffee, he went straight to the kitchen. Then the cry went out.

'Where are my hot cross buns?'

Appearing somewhat surprised, I replied, 'You left them on the kitchen worktop!'

'Well they're not here now.' Then there was a slight pause. 'The bag is in the bin and it's empty!' he said. 'Has someone been in here?'

'Only big Andy Murphy!' I said, somewhat nonchalantly. 'He called in for a quick cup of tea and said something about "These hot cross buns are crying out to be eaten", but I told him he better not and to leave them down!'

'The greedy big bastard, he's only gone and eaten them both.'

After some really hot cross words, he calmed down with a jam doughnut and a cup of hot coffee, the wee soul!

However, I had great pleasure in contacting Andy and informing him of what he had done and I even convinced him that I said, 'Well you'd better not and to leave them down!'

Suffice to say, we received a daily delivery to the office for a whole week of donuts, chocolate éclairs, scones and buns from an apologetic, arse-licking Andy, trying desperately to get back in favour with the sergeant!

However, I forgot to mention to big arse-licking Andy that the hot cross sergeant was off that week on annual leave!

Ming-night in Moscow

. . .

I have a serious problem which I will share with you and it's this: no matter where I go abroad, my arse touches down in that country before the aeroplane does.

A laxative to me is a Thomas Cook travel brochure: as soon as I begin viewing it the cheeks of my bum start opening and shutting like a set of elevator doors at the Hilton Hotel!

Such was the case when, as a member of a Scottish folk band, I was touring Moscow in Russia.

The morning after our arrival, I was uplifted by the tour organiser and taken to view our first concert venue.

He took me to the impressive Moskvitch Centre, where I saw our band's name in six-feet lettering at the top of the building, and picture posters of us displayed in every window around the main entrance with 'Sold Out' signs prominently displayed alongside them.

I was shown around the stage area, which appeared to go back and back and back – you could have held a football match on this stage – and the bottom tier of the venue, which housed twelve hundred seats, with a further eight hundred above that.

This was a plush venue, but I had to curtail my sightseeing tour as my stomach started to react to my new surroundings and I sensed I was about to give birth to something resembling an avalanche!

With very little time to spare, I asked my tour organiser to direct me to the nearest available toilet, pronto!

'Dimitri!' he called out, and an older man appeared, who he then conversed with in Russian. When finished, he turned to me and said, 'You must follow him, Harry!'

That said, I was off following after my new guide, who led me along several corridors before stopping at a door.

Using sign language, he signalled for me to remain outside.

As I waited, I watched him through the glass door as he fumbled his way through several keys until he found the right one to open a drawer on the office desk.

He then unhooked a small key from inside the drawer, which he placed in his breast pocket, before closing and locking the drawer with his key and returning to me.

'Follow! Follow!' he repeated, like an old Rangers supporter.

As off we went again along the corridor, with me desperately holding the arse of my trousers and walking like Lily Savage in a tight dress!

What seemed like several miles later, and with my legs being held so tightly together as to produce enough chaffing between my thighs to start a fire, we eventually reached a toilet.

Having looked at the severe anguish and agony etched across my face, the guide opened the door and stood clear as I burst through it like a drug officer on a raid.

I quickly dropped my kegs and was about to position my big jazz drum over the toilet hole and relax the tension to open my bomb doors when I happened to glance down and saw the most bogging toilet I have ever encountered – and I've been to some toilets in the Barrowfield that really take the biscuit!

I immediately screeched to a halt before I made initial contact with the seat and stood up straight again, closing my bomb doors in the same movement.

The smell emanating from the toilet pan was so bad I

thought I had entered Lenin's tomb or, as he was referred to by the younger Russians, 'Old Foostie'.

It was stinging my eyes and, as I strained to focus on it, I noticed half the toilet seat had either rotted away and fell off, or had been eaten by whatever was hiding in there.

The toilet paper was torn pieces of old newspaper, which were saturated in urine and stained brown in colour.

As desperate as I was to empty my bowels, there was no way my clean bum was touching this seat and, more importantly, I was more worried about what might have crawled up my bare arse if I sat down, rather than what might have dropped out of it.

As quickly as I entered the toilet I was up and out, faster than a speeding bullet, shuffling my way along the corridors to my waiting tour operator, and I didn't even wait for Dimitri to replace the special key in the drawer.

Later, when I returned to the luxury of my toilet within the Grand Marriott Hotel, I thought to myself, 'The only reason to lock that toilet door was surely to keep the smell in!'

Which reminds me of a story about a guy who went to the doctor's surgery for an examination and the doctor said to him, 'I'm sorry to inform you of this, but you have a severe case of the crabs!'

Quick as a flash, the guy says, 'I must have caught them off a toilet seat!'

To which the doctor responded by saying, 'Well you must have been eating the seat then, because you have them in your mouth!'

He was last seen walking sideways out the doctor's surgery.

A Friendly Game

· · ·

A popular sport played by many serving police officers and recommended for relieving stress and providing excellent relaxation and harmony amongst the participants is golf.

The following is a very short story related to me by a colleague.

It was a sunny Monday morning on the first hole of a busy course and Derek was beginning his pre-shot routine, visualising his upcoming shot, when a piercing voice bellowed out from the clubhouse loudspeaker, 'Would the gentleman on the ladies' tee back up to the men's tee, please!'

Derek could feel every eye on the course looking at him, but was still deep into his routine, like a professional, seemingly impervious to the interruption. Again the announcer broadcast, 'Would the gentleman on the ladies' tee kindly back up to the men's tee!'

Derek simply ignored the announcement and kept concentrating, when once again, the announcer called out, 'Would the gentleman on the ladies' tee, back up to the men's tee, please!'

This was the final straw for Derek, who stopped, looked over at the clubhouse window directly at the announcer (who was still holding the microphone up to his mouth) and shouted back, 'Would the bastard in the clubhouse holding the mike kindly shut the fuck up and let me concentrate on my second shot!'

The Square Go

• • •

Along with Alex Sterrick, I attended a call to the Wynford area of Maryhill regarding a domestic disturbance within a house.

On our arrival we were met by an elderly Irish woman who informed us that her nineteen-year-old son had been abusing drugs and alcohol and had started an argument with her, resulting in him becoming aggressive toward her, pushing her about and smashing the front glass door to the house.

Fearful for her safety, she had ordered him to leave the house, but the son subjected her to threats of physical violence, before brushing her aside and going upstairs to his bedroom.

Having endured this type of behaviour over a long period, she'd had enough and decided there was no other alternative but to have him removed from the house, although she pleaded with me not to arrest him because he would come back and hit her.

After noting the complaint and the vandalism caused to the front door, we went upstairs to confront the son and try the softly, softly approach.

As I knocked on the bedroom door, a voice called out, 'Fuck off back to your farm, pig! I know it's you!'

I took this remark as a term of endearment and an invitation to enter the room.

The son was covered up in his bed, so I informed him why I was there and to get dressed and come down the stairs with us, as his mother wanted him to leave the house.

After some initial verbal and physical resistance,

whereby the son threatened me and challenged me to an 'old fashioned square go', where you both engage in a fight with no weapons or any other persons involved (I declined his offer), and removed him with some force from the family home.

'Cannae handle it, eh? Ye're a big man when there's two o' you, but ye cannae dae it yersel', too feart that I'll batter ye!' he said.

These aggressive and challenging taunts continued and were mirrored in his body language, as he beckoned me to come ahead when I ordered him to move away from the front of his mother's house.

Having endured his threatening hard man behaviour long enough I agreed to his request. 'Well, if you really believe that sonny, why don't you walk down the road a bit and I'll follow you through a back close and we'll have a square go!' I responded.

As he walked down the road, away from his mother's house, I followed after him slowly until we arrived at a quiet spot, at which point I signalled to him which back-court to enter.

At that, he began gesticulating with his hands and shouting abusive remarks at me, 'Away an' fuck yersel', ya big diddy!' Before running off.

Several people appeared at windows on hearing the disturbance.

Having taken enough threats and verbal abuse from this woman-hitting hard man, I gave chase after him.

After a short distance through backcourts and gardens he stumbled and fell to the ground, allowing me to catch up and apprehend him.

I then placed him in the rear of the police vehicle and

removed him to the old Maryhill Police Office in Gairbraid Avenue, Glasgow.

As we stood in the line at the charge bar, he was mouthing off to others around him.

'Right! Next accused,' called out the duty officer, Inspector Joyce.

Alex and I approached the bar with our prisoner and I charged him with the disturbance.

The duty officer took note of it, before turning to the accused and asking him, 'Do you wish to make any reply to the charge?'

The accused said, 'Aye, I do!' He then continued, 'I would just like tae tell ye, that Starsky and Hutch here offered me a square go and when I refused to fight, they gave me the jail!'

To which the duty officer responded by picking up his wooden desk ruler and saying, 'Oh don't be so ridiculous, son. Polis don't go around offering neds a square go. Then he paused for a moment, before adding, 'We just batter fuck out of you!'

At that, he then hit the accused a dull yin across the head with his wooden ruler, then said, 'Lock this wee wimp up!'

Die(t) at Craigie Street

· · ·

Many an accused person that I arrested in the south side of Glasgow would ask you to take them to Govan, or any other office for that matter, complaining about the prisoner meals served up by the female turnkey officer responsible for feeding them while in our custody.

I would never succumb to their request, but I was later to realise why I was continually asked.

It was during a stint as a bar officer within Craigie Street Police Office, where I was responsible for checking the prisoners in my custody and making the female turnkey aware of how many of them were being detained and therefore required a meal.

It was a perk of the job that, if you wanted a cooked meal from her, you just let her know and she cooked you a meal at the same time.

Most other turnkeys at the various other police stations would do the easy thing and send out to the local chip shop for fish and chips or sausage and chips to feed them, thereby using up the allowance they were allocated to spend on each prisoners meal. However, Cathy Carberry, my specific turnkey, didn't agree to this and would insist in providing the prisoners in our care with some home-made food!

By doing this she could make money off the subsistence allowance allocated to feed them by cooking for them in bulk.

I walked into her kitchen and interrupted her during the preparation of one of her so-called home-made dinners.

'That's another two prisoners just been locked up,

Cathy, and the duty officer wants them fed, so that'll be nine you now have for dinner,' I informed her.

As I made her aware of our updated guest list, I glanced down at the plastic plates spread out on her kitchen table.

Each contained two slices of some sort of meat which I could only describe as resembling reject skin grafts from Canniesburn Hospital. It was that thin, I even had to touched it to make sure it wasn't a photocopy she had thrown onto the plates.

The token amount of frozen potato chips spread around the plates couldn't hide the fact that the bottom of the plate was blue and, to crown it all off, she had a pot of baked beans bubbling away on the gas ring.

'Well that's aw the frozen chips I have and I'm no' going out to the shops to buy any mer'. And I'm buggered if I'm opening another tin o' spam for them either!'

At that, she leaned over the table and began to lift chips from the plates she had previously set out and placed them onto the two extra plates, spreading them out sparingly in an effort to make the plate look busy.

She then lifted the skin grafts she had prepared earlier off each plate in turn and ripped a piece off to add to the new plates.

Finally, Cathy finished them off by counting the number of chips on each plate, making sure they were all equal with fourteen each and breaking in half any bigger chips, before dumping a spoonful of hot bubbling baked beans over them all just to add a splash of colour and supplement the prisoners' protein intake!

She put the loaves and fishes feast to shame by her distribution methods.

The final piece of Cathy's culinary cuisine came in the

shape of a faded plastic blue mug and a slice of pan bread – a basic loaf from Tesco, at a cost of about 15 pence – with a scraping of cheap margarine.

Now we are not talking Jamie Oliver here. But *Oliver*, maybe. Gruel most definitely!

'I don't think I'm gonnae have enough tae feed you as well Harry!' she said apologetically.

'Don't worry about me, Cathy, I'll just get a greasy fish supper out of Marini's chippie on the Main Street and think of what I might have had!' I replied.

Although I really wanted to say, 'Thank you, Lord!'

'Will ye help me feed them?' she asked as she poured what she described as their tea into their plastic mugs.

Some of the prisoners had been locked up all day and were so hungry, they would have eaten a scabby cat 'atween two slices o' stale bread, but some of the others were more sceptical and asked, 'Hey, big man, whit the fuck is this ye're givin' me?'

'It's yer dinner!' I replied sympathetically.

'My dinner? I got the fuckin' jail last night 'cause ah hit my wife for giving a plate o' grub that was better than this lot!' came back the reply, before they continued, 'Who's in the kitchen tonight, Fanny Craddock or that other fanny wi' his Atkins diet?'

However, the plastic mug of tea was the icing on the cake for many a prisoner that night.

'Whit is this pish ye're givin' us now, big yin?' I was asked by a prisoner, staring into his mug like a clairvoyant.

'It's yer tea!' I replied, somewhat hesitantly.

He looked at it intently for a moment and said, 'Fuck me, big man, but when I was as weak as that, my wee mammy would sit up all night tae nurse me! There isnae any tea leaves in my mug tae see ma future!

'Whoever came up wi' that load o' crap and called it a meal must work for the government, 'cause as long as ye're dishing oot that load o' shit for prisoners' grub, ye'll no' need tae bring back hanging as a deterrent!'

Sympathy from the Abbey

· · ·

I fully understand and wholeheartedly respect the recent trend for friends, neighbours and relatives to express their compassion for a lost loved one by placing bouquets of flowers, pictures, scarves and shirts at the scene of their loss. But – with all due respect to those tragically killed in an accident, murdered or who, unfortunately, just happen to drop down dead due to a serious illness – the other night, while watching the news on television, I couldn't help but smile.

Here was the BBC News reporter relating the serious story of another horrific and unfortunate death of a member of the public in a Glasgow housing scheme, when the cameraman focused down on the very spot where the victim's dead body had fallen after he had been callously slain.

The body had been removed (well obviously, Harry) and the many tributes mentioned, such as flowers, scarves and football shirts, now adorned the location, but I couldn't help but raise a smile at the lone half bottle of Buckfast tonic wine situated prominently at the front of all the colourful condolence cards.

This could only be Glasgow!

Old Firm Day

...

Like every workplace in the west of Scotland, friendly banter was the order of the day at the police office following an Old Firm derby match between the two giants of Glasgow football, Rangers and Celtic.

'That was never an offside – he was clearly onside. A man wi' a white stick and a guide dog could see that!' said one officer.

'Don't talk such rubbish! He was a mile off!' argued another.

'Bollocks! It's obvious that the linesman was a biased hun!'

The linesman referred to, who dared raise his flag for such a decision, just happened to be a uniformed police officer and an up and coming part-time grade one referee.

As the temperature became raised in the dispute and the heated arguments got louder, the door to the CID office burst open and in marched Detective Inspector Lyall holding to his chest an enlarged photocopy of a daily newspaper showing the said polis linesman and whistling the tune to *The Sash*.

As he marched along the length of the office, past all of the detective officers seated at their desks, each in turn saw the funny side of his intervention and burst out laughing as he about turned and marched right out again, closing the door behind him.

However, someone didn't see the funny side and complained when DI Lyall jokingly made up a mock recommendation that the said polis linesman be awarded a high commendation by the chief constable for his display of extreme bravery and the complete disregard for his own safety in disallowing a perfectly good goal for Celtic!

Luxuries of Life

. . .

Whilst working in the warrant section, I came across a sheriff apprehension warrant for a male residing in Ferguslie Park Avenue in Paisley.

With such a posh-sounding name for his address, curiosity got the better of me and I decided to pay him a visit and execute the warrant.

Armed with my A-to-Z street guide, I made my way to Paisley and the Ferguslie Park area.

Boy, oh boy! How wrong was I, as I turned off the motorway for the posh area that I had imagined, only discovering it to be the Paisley Town Council's housing scheme answer to downtown Baghdad! It was like a bomb-site!

There were stray dogs running around in packs; the odd burnt-out, abandoned stolen car, stripped of any useful bits before being set alight by the local joyriders; supermarket trolleys lining the roadway where trees once blossomed, adding some much needed greenery to a rather dull and depressing area; and the place was littered with empty houses boarded up by the council. Whether that was designed to keep people out or keep them in, I'm not quite sure.

Suffice to say, when I came across some life in the area in the shape of three men walking together, it turned out that one of them was handcuffed and the other two were plain-clothes police officers.

After several minutes of driving around and forming the obvious comparisons with Ruchazie, Drumchapel and Blackhill in Glasgow, I came across the address I was seeking.

Right up in the tenement close building, I knocked on the outside door to the house.

Several moments later, the door was answered by a rough-looking male in his mid-fifties. Rough in as much as he was unshaven, unwashed and unkempt in his appearance.

'Can I speak with David Ferguson, please?' I asked him.

'Nae chance pal, unless ye can dae it through a medium!' he replied.

'What do you mean?' I asked him.

'He died a week past Tuesday while eating a fish supper and two pickled onions,' he replied in all seriousness. 'I've kept the *Paisley Express* newspaper wi' the story in it. D'ye want tae see it for yersel'?' he added.

I paused for a moment while digesting what he had just said. 'He died eating a fish supper?' I asked in amazement, expecting to be informed that he had choked on a fish bone!

'And two pickled onions!' he added, as if they were significant in the cause of his death.

'If ye don't mind, yes, I would like to see the paper!' I responded.

'Well ye better come on in,' he said, opening the door wider and beckoning us to follow him. 'Just watch yer feet, the dog had a wee accident this morning.'

I wondered why my colleague hesitated, but soon realised when I looked down at the floor and saw that the entire length of the hallway was littered with dog dirt.

Despite having very little sense of smell, due to having damaged my nose on numerous occasions, the stench emanating from it was so strong it was stinging my eyes and my partner, who possessed an excellent sense of smell, made his excuses in order to remain at the outside door.

I followed my guide's every step as he negotiated the treacherous minefield before us, making certain I did not divert in any way from his well-trodden route, and taking exceptional notice of any newly deposited steaming piles.

I also noticed that the soles of my boots were sticking to the wooden floor and I immediately began thinking about my exit back out onto the street and the need to clean them thoroughly. This was one house where you definitely wiped your feet on the road out!

Reaching the end of the hallway, I entered the living-room area.

'There ye go, big yin! Read it for yersel'. Front-page story,' he said, handing me the newspaper. 'The only time I ever got my name in the paper, wis when the Council held a warrant sale at the house tae get their rent money!'

I focused on the newspaper headline. It read:

'PAISLEY MAN KILLED IN FATAL ROAD ACCIDENT!'

I turned to my informer and said, 'It says here, he was killed in a road accident!'

'Correct! But the reason he got blootered wi' the taxi, was because he stepped oot onto the road, wi' his heid doon, eating his fish supper and two pickled onions. He'd only just left the chippie and it wis still hot, tae!' he replied sincerely. 'It turns oot, he had phoned for a taxi tae take him up the road and got fed up waiting, so he decided to walk hame eating his fish supper. Crossed o'er the road while munching away and the rest is history.

'And afore ye ask . . . Naw, it wisnae his taxi!'

As I stood there with my feet stuck firmly to the wooden

floorboards, surveying the emptiness of the room – it completely lacked any furniture apart from an extremely large thirty-inch coloured television on a stand broadcasting horse racing, a green plastic patio chair positioned in front of it, an empty wooden box used as a table for his tobacco, cigarette papers and ashtray to sit on and, taking up pride of place, the 'patron saint of Easterhouse' in the shape of a framed colour print of the lovely Suzie Wong hanging from the spacious living room wall.

One automatically thinks, 'All the comforts of home required!'

'Where's all yer furniture?' I enquired.

'You've noticed then?' he said. 'Never trust the opposite sex. I went tae the bookies tae put a line oan and when I got back, she had emptied the entire hoose – this was aw she had bloody left me with, the cow!'

'Well at least she left ye with the telly to watch.' I said trying to commiserate with him.

'Aye! Only because her two brothers couldnae lift it man, it weighs a bloody ton!'

'Well it would do, wi' all those horses on it every day.' I said facetiously.

'Aye right, pal, dae a look daft?' he said.

At which point, I couldn't resist asking, 'Tell me this. Where do you come from originally, mate?'

Quick as a flash came back the reply I was expecting, 'Glesca of course!'

Ye're a Tube

· · ·

Several years ago, I had occasion to attend at my doctor's surgery, with a particularly delicate male complaint.

'Okay, Mr Morris! Drop your trousers and lie on the couch,' she said with such a voice of authority that I immediately responded to her command.

'Right, let's see what the problem is today!' she continued, pulling on her Molly Maid plastic gloves, and beginning to fondle – sorry, examine! my testicles ever so gently.

After a few moments, she stood up, began to rip off her gloves and gave me a look of disgust as she uttered the words, 'Not a bump, lump, plook or pimple, Mr Morris!'

'Are ye sure doctor? Would you no' like to re-examine me once more?' I asked her . . . Well, pleaded with her!

'No, Mr Morris, I wouldn't like to re-examine you! I've already examined you four times this week for the same complaint and can find nothing. No lumps, no bumps! Nothing!

'You are becoming what is referred to in the British Medical Journal as a TUBE!' she exclaimed.

'Hoh, doctor! I think you're a bit out of order with that remark!' I replied, displaying my annoyance.

To which she responded immediately, 'I am referring to your daily appointments for the same procedure Mr Morris, which are Totally Unnecessary Bollock Examinations! Hence the expression, you're a TUBE!'

Donald Lindsay
and Reminsky

• • •

The door of the front office opened and in walked Donald Lindsay, a former colleague and now a retired from the force for several years.

'Hello, Donald!' I said, putting my hand out to shake his. 'And how are you, mate?' I asked sincerely.

He gave me a blank, vacant look and said, 'Do you know me, mister?'

'Of course I do, Donald! It's me, Harry Morris. We worked together. Surely you remember me?'

That reply went right over the top of Donald's head, and he said, 'I can't find my gloves and I need to wear them when it's cold or my hands get sore!'

I quickly realised that Donald was ill and within a very short time I learned that he was missing from a south-side nursing home, where he was being treated for dementia.

As I sat with Donald, keeping him occupied, while awaiting the arrival of staff from the home, I thought back to our days at Craigie Street Police Office, where Donald had spent most of his service, and how I always looked upon him as a very smart, polite and knowledgeable officer, who I searched out on numerous occasions to ask for advice on police matters.

On one occasion, when I had been fortunate enough to be partnered with Donald while we worked in the divisional crime car, he related this story to me about one of the best known criminal safe crackers in Britain, 'Gentleman' Johnny Reminsky, who he had the task, along with his partner Bert Gorman, of escorting from Glasgow

High Court to Peterhead Prison after his final appearance at court on an appeal against his sentence.

Referred to as 'Gentleman' Johnny because he was never violent, his crimes were that of breaking into premises and opening their safes and removing the contents!

He performed the art of safe breaking rather well. In fact, rather too well: his handiwork was instantly recognisable and he was consequently arrested within a few days of the crime being discovered.

During his brief appearance for his appeal, he was allowed a visit from his family, before being placed in the police car and driven off on the long journey back up to Peterhead Prison.

It was during the long and tedious journey in heavy traffic that they decided to stop for a break and change of driver.

Johnny had intimated he was dying for a drink and also required to visit the toilet.

Donald pulled into the car park of a Country Tavern and, as they were about to apply the handcuffs on Johnny in order to convey him inside to the toilets, Johnny said in his Polish accent, 'Here, guys, why do you have to do this to me when I need to piss? Why you not let me go in myself without you and your uniforms and I will buy the drinks also for us to enjoy?'

Donald and Bert looked at each other and deliberated for a moment. They knew they could not enter the licensed premises in uniform and enjoy the thirst quenching delights of a cool beer.

In the short time they had spent together with Johnny, they had developed a mutual respect, and Johnny always displayed the utmost admiration for the police and the difficult job they performed.

'Trust me!' said Johnny, one of Britain's most famous criminals thanks to his renowned exploits during the war. 'I will not do anything to get you guys into trouble.'

Donald and Bert looked at each other again before agreeing to his request. After all, it would be the last time Johnny would visit a pub for a very long time.

'Okay!' said Donald. 'Here's some money to buy the beers, but don't let us down, Johnny!' he pleaded with him.

'Don't worry, I will be right out!' he replied as he took possession of the money. He then walked towards the door of the tavern and disappeared inside.

Bert quickly rushed over to a window at the side of the tavern to try and observe what was taking place inside.

Soon Johnny appeared, larger than life, walking like a free man, albeit briefly free, from the door of the tavern, carrying three tins of pale ale.

As he entered the unmarked police car, he handed them over to Donald.

'There you are, sir!' said Johnny. 'That wasn't long.'

As Donald took possession of the beers, a disappointed look came over his face, and he turned towards Bert. 'Tin opener! No tin opener. How are we going to open them?'

'Not a problem,' said Johnny, as he placed his hand in his jacket pocket and handed over a small metal tin opener. 'It was lying on the bar just asking to be lifted!'

'Johnny!' said Donald. 'You'll get us all the jail for stealing!' Taking it from him, he opened each tin and handed them out. 'Ahhh! That's brilliant, but in all honesty, I would have preferred to drink it from a cool pint glass, rather than a tin!'

No sooner had Donald uttered these words than Johnny produced two pint tumblers from the inside pocket of his jacket.

As Donald and Bert looked at him for an explanation, Johnny replied dismissively, 'They were also lying on the bar just asking to be lifted!'

Enough is Enough!

· · ·

An elderly male appeared at court on a charge concerning sex in a public place.

'Are you John Thomas?' asked the procurator fiscal.

As he was about to answer, the accused suffered a coughing fit. '*Cough! Cough! Cough!* Correct, sir!' he replied.

'And do you reside at 43 Molendinar Street, in Glasgow?'

Again, the accused began coughing as he tried to answer. '*Cough! Cough! Cough!* Correct again, sir!' he replied.

'Mr Thomas, let us cut to the chase, as they say. Were you performing a sexual act on another male within a public toilet in Queen's Park on Monday 14th February, when you were arrested by plain clothes police officers?'

As the accused tried to answer, he began coughing and spluttering uncontrollably. '*Cough! Cough! Cough!* . . . *Cough! Cough! Cough!*'

At this point the sheriff intervened and said to the accused, 'That's a terrible cough you've got. Have you tried sucking a Fisherman's Friend?'

To which the accused replied, 'With all due respect, m'lord, that's exactly what I was doing when I was arrested in the first place!'

Bird Shit!

. . .

One day, we were sitting outside a friend's motor garage, soaking up the sun and eating our lunch of cooked chicken drumsticks supplied by one of his customers.

As we sat there munching away, my friend Bobby threw the bone from one of his drumsticks onto the roadway and, within seconds, a large seagull appeared from nowhere, swooped down and lifted it cleanly off the roadway.

It then flew off with it, swallowing it down whole at the same time.

'Did you see that?' Bobby shouted excitedly. 'Watch this.'

This time he threw a whole drumstick leg onto the roadway and, again, within seconds of it landing a seagull appeared, swooped down to pick it up and swallowed it down whole, bones and all.

After Bobby had performed this act of discarding half-eaten chicken drumsticks onto the roadway several times, the Bridgeton area resembled a scene from Alfred Hitchcock's thriller *The Birds*, having attracted more seagulls than there are in Saltcoats.

'You better bring yer motor inside. It'll be much safer, Harry!'

'Safer from what?' I asked him, surprised by his remark.

To which he replied in all sincerity, 'From they big basterting seagulls, 'cause efter whit they just swallowed, if they start shitting on yer motor, they're liable to smash yer fuckin' windscreen!'

Line-Up for Trouble

· · ·

When I was a member of the court branch in Glasgow, one of my least favourite duties came late in the afternoon, when all available police officers not busy with their daily court duties would attend the Glasgow sheriff court cells to perform duty on 'the cutter'!

Now the cutter, as it was known, was when all the prisoners who had been arrested the night before made their first appearance in court in front of a sheriff and pled either guilty or not guilty to the charge levelled against them.

If guilty, they were dealt with there and then. If not guilty, they were given a time and date to reappear at the court.

The way this duty was performed was as follows:

The court/bar officer would allocate you with a prisoner name and cell number. You would then go to the police officer in charge of the cells, referred to as the 'turnkey', informing him of your prisoner and his cell number. He in turn would fetch your prisoner from the cell for you.

You would then escort your prisoner to a holding cell/detention room at the side door of the court, where he was detained until his number was called as the next accused to appear.

During this time you would take a seat on one of the uncomfortable corridor benches and wait your turn but, when there were forty or fifty accused to go through the court, you often had a long wait.

One day, I was sitting there totally bored with this duty. Another police officer was waiting with his prisoner by the door of the court for the present accused to come out so that he could enter and continue the process. It operated like a conveyor belt, time being of the essence.

This particular accused had shaved his long hair off at the sides of his head with the rest tied back in a ponytail, with a thick Mexican-style moustache that covered his mouth and a large visible hole in his nose where a nut and bolt piercing usually stayed.

He was also about six foot five inches in height, wearing tight denims and cowboy boots, with a sleeveless body-warmer jacket exposing his bare arms, which were littered with colourful tattoos of daggers, bloody hearts and evil symbols of devil worship.

As he stood in line, he was mouthing off about certain prisoners and what he was going to do to them and boasting that it took several baton-wielding police officers to arrest him.

He continued in this vein, until a few others and I got totally fed up listening to his continual ranting and berating of the police, so I said, 'Hoh, gattling gub! Why don't you shut the fuck up and maybe everybody will just *think* yer an asshole, instead of opening yer big stupid mouth and confirming it for them!'

He looked over and focussed his evil eyes on me, while digesting what I had just said. Then, suddenly, he went totally ballistic and hurled himself at me screaming obscenities.

I immediately bent my knees up and kicked out at him, hitting him in the chest, but his momentum and his eager-ness to get to me propelled him on and he grabbed hold of me, his charge culminating in both of us ending up on the cell passage floor.

At that, several of the police officers sitting in the

corridor came to my assistance and after an almighty struggle we physically restrained him. But he hadn't been joking about the number of us that had been required the night before to do so.

Eventually, handcuffed and in our control, he was dragged back to his cell kicking and screaming abuse.

Afterwards, I was taken aside by the court/bar officer and told, 'We've taken all morning to calm that big evil bastard down. We even asked the casualty surgeon to prescribe him Valium and within two fuckin' minutes of meeting you, all hell's broken out and it's World War III in the cell passage.

'So! Do me a favour, Harry. Keep your fuckin' opinions and remarks to yourself and don't upset any more of my prisoners!'

Which makes you think some cops just take the job a bit too seriously!

Offer I Had to Refuse
· · ·

My elderly next door neighbour is a keen wild bird enthusiast and had put up some impressive nesting bird boxes, which were very quickly occupied. Excited at the prospect of the birds nesting, she called at my house and said, 'If you're not too busy Harry, would you like to come next door and take a look at my blue tits?'

A purple rinse and blue tits!

How does one respond to that? Fortunately, I said I was married!

Forgot Me Already?

. . .

I don't think this sort of thing is only familiar to me: I'm sure we have all encountered something similar in our time.

I came home the other day and I was checking through my answer machine messages, when all of a sudden: 'Message 4'.

'Harry! It's yer mother calling you! I'm on the telephone in my house. Are you in your house, or are you out again? I've noticed you are out a lot recently. Why don't you call over to my house the next time you're out and visit me? Yer mother. I'm in . . . '

At that point, she stopped talking and I could hear her doorbell ringing and then I recognised my voice in the background shouting, 'Hello! Are you in, Mam? It's me, Harry.'

And so my mother, still being recorded on my telephone answering machine I might add, says to me, 'Oh it's you Harry! I was just calling you.'

Then she whispers quietly into the telephone, 'I'll call you back after, son, when you get home!'

Then there was a pause before she added, still whispering, 'That was you that just walked in to my house!'

Then she couldn't resist adding, 'By the way! I can't believe that you're out again! You ought to stay in sometime and answer your blooming phone!'

Ch-Ch-Ch-Changes

. . .

I was working with a police colleague on a shift prior to her wedding and she was relating her fears of getting to the church and making a mistake, like forgetting her words or tripping up. So, as a fatherly figure, I gave her my expert advice.

'Right, Jackie!' I said. 'Firstly, you enter through the church doors and the first thing you want to focus on is the aisle, which you're going to walk down.'

'Right! The aisle. I'm walking down the aisle,' she said.

'Second thing you'll focus on is the altar – that is where you're heading for. The altar is where you need to be.'

'Okay! The altar is next. I'm walking down the aisle and I'm heading for the altar where I need to be. Got you! What's next?' she asked me, eagerly wanting to know.

'Finally, it's him. You stand next to him.'

'So! Let me get this right. I walk down the aisle, toward the altar and stand next to him, my future husband!'

'That's it, Jackie, you've got it,' I said, pleased with my advice.

The big day of her wedding arrived and as I stood there watching the bride being led by her proud father into the church, all I could hear as she passed was Jackie saying over and over again, 'Aisle, altar, him! Aisle, altar, him! Aisle, altar, him!'

Personally, I never knew what it was like to sleep myself until I got married!

A Coloured TV in Govan

. . .

A good friend who joined the police with me was Jimmy Clark. He was a housing scheme boy like myself and possessed two of the most important ingredients in the make up of a good police officer – common sense and a sense of humour!

The latter was to prove invaluable when he and his wife decided it was time to move house and find something with more room for their two boys, Dominic and Martin.

Having secured the new house they wanted in the plush Croftfoot area, Jimmy set about decorating his flat in the Govan area of Glasgow in order to make it desirable to some first time home buyers, with two such couples having expressed an interest in seeing it with a view to buying.

Tricia specially picked the new autumn paint colour scheme required to brighten it up, then she left for the day, along with the boys, to allow Jimmy the peace and time he needed to perform his magic with the paintbrush and roller.

All day long Jimmy sweated buckets as he moved items of furniture about the rooms in order to decorate the walls and skirting boards, Finally, he was left with just one wall, already given its first coat of paint.

Tricia returned to the flat and was so impressed with the result of Jimmy's efforts that she contemplated buying it herself!

With the boys fed and packed off to bed, it was time for Jimmy to add the final finishing touches and give the second coat of paint to the last wall in the lounge.

About 3 a.m. the following morning, he finally finished the job.

Tired and weary from his marathon of decorating, he plonked the brush and roller down, washed the excess paint off his hands and retired, somewhat knackered, to his bed, convinced he had completed the transformation to his flat's colour scheme that would prove totally irresistible to the prospective buyers who would be arriving to view it later the same day.

Lying peacefully in a relaxing, restful sleep, Jimmy and Tricia were aroused by fits of laughter and giggles coming from Dominic and Martin who were in the lounge area of the flat.

They lay there half awake thinking how much the boys enjoyed each other's company and what a big difference a move to a bigger house would be for the entire family.

After a short while, Tricia decided to get up out of bed and go through to the lounge and view Jimmy's finished work.

As she entered the room, she was completely speechless for several moments, as she took in all before her.

'Jimmy! Quick! Come and see this!'

Jimmy jumped out of his bed in a panic and immediately went through to check what was wrong.

There, sitting in the middle of the lounge floor, covered from head to toe in the orange Autumn paint, having daubed each other thoroughly, were Dominic and Martin, blending in perfectly with the orange coffee table, the orange sideboard, both arms of the orange sofa and the previously black and white, now orange television set (making it one of the first colour TVs in Govan).

Surely this was the birth of the original concept for the popular TV programme *Changing Rooms* – only instead of Carol Smillie we would have had Tricia Clark and instead of Laurence Llewelyn Bowen we'd have Jimmy Clark in a baggy police shirt, with their family of interior designers, Dominic and Martin Clark!

Who would have believed a famous slogan was born in Govan? 'The future's bright! The future's Orange!'

Bruised and Battered
without the Bevy
· · ·

The other night, I was sitting watching Paul McKenna working his magic on all those who like to eat to excess.

He was giving them all sorts of advice of how to overcome their obsession and their craving for food.

'When you feel the urge to get up and go to the kitchen for that can of coke or that chocolate biscuit, just start tapping on several pressure point areas around your face and body. I want you to continue doing it until the craving and obsessive urge goes away!'

I felt like a wee whisky, so I decided to try out the Paul McKenna tapping remedy to curb my drinking habit.

I tapped my face and body for that long and that hard, when I eventually awakened from my unconscious state my face was so swollen and bruised I looked like I had been beaten up by Mike Tyson!

Thanks for the advice, Paul, but I think I'll stick to my whisky!

The Dyslexic Reporter

• • •

Brian Graham was a very clever, well-educated guy, as well as a big fat, greedy bugger who ate for Britain.

When he heard that a certain sergeant whom he disliked was coming to our shift he decided to set him up and wanted some of us to help him convince the new sergeant that he was dyslexic.

This he did by submitting the following written police report for him to check, which took the sergeant the entire week to decipher.

Police Report

Ta mite, hate ant focus, I war hen caged no toad parole, then I sad ovation do spot a bar seeing rivend among het toad.

No peakings wits het diver, me confined seeing het woner.

Feart I sad woken wits hit, I reformed hit what hi saw seeing changed wits feeling do dismay a fax dish.

Me male on deeply ant saw hallowed do so.

I ban intensify het accrued.

Translated

At time, date and locus, I was engaged on road patrol, when I had occasion to stop a car being driven along the road.

On speaking with the driver, he confirmed being the owner.

After I had spoken with him, I informed him that he was being charged with failing to display a tax disc.

He made no reply and was allowed to go.

I can identify the accused.

'On tother a ball, how you know when!' **I think!**

Ringing From The Waist Down

· · ·

'Flora! Flora!' a haunting, pitiful, wailing voice bellowed out late at night.

'Aw shit! It's yer drunken faither. Quick! Ye better get into yer beds oot o' his way!'

His cries for my mother Flora got louder and more pitiful.

'Flora! For fuck's sakes Flora, will ye come and help me? I'm soaking wet. I might drown in this water!'

'No such luck!' she said under her breath, as she stepped out from the house into the backcourt. 'Where are ye? I cannae see anything, it's too dark.'

'I'm over here!' he called out again. 'I'm waving my erms at ye like a maniac.'

'Ye could be dancin' the Slosh for all I know, but whit are ye dayin' in the burn ya stupit big bugger?' she shouted.

'Well it's no' the bloody breast stroke, that's for sure, 'cause I cannae swim, so gonnae get o'er here and gie's a haun tae get oot afore I droon, I'm bloody freezin!' he pleaded.

There he was, on an October-chilled night, soaked to the skin with the icy cold water of the local burn, as it weaved its winding way along the rear of our backcourt on it's way to eventually becoming part of the River Clyde.

Minus several gallons of it, which had been soaked up by my father's brand new Arran jumper that my granny in Govan knitted for him.

'I cannae believe you were in the navy during the war and ye cannae even swim. Mind you, from whit you've telt me, the biggest majority o' the British navy couldnae swim.

'God help us! If Hitler had known that, he would have just challenged us tae a swimming gala instead of having to fight us!

'In saying that, we'd have probably suffered more casualties through drowning.'

She paused for a moment, before reaching out her hand to grab hold of his.

'Noo! If Hitler had challenged ye tae drinking that would have been a different story, the war would have been over within six days, never mind six years!'

'Gonnae gie yer gums a rest and jist pull me oot o' here?' responded my dad.

When my mam eventually got him into the house she helped him off with his wet clothes, while dipping his trouser pockets of any loose change that the local barman had missed.

As she put her hand into his pocket, she pulled out a handful of thick gooey slime.

'Whit the hell is this?' she asked him.

'Frogs' spawn!' he replied, pleased with himself. 'I got it for the weans!'

'I've heard o' some people falling into the Clyde and emerging with a salmon in their pocket, but you emerge wi' a haun full o' bloody slime,' she said disgustedly, shaking it from her hand.

'Flora hen! Whit's for my dinner? I'm starving,' he asked her pleadingly.

Quick as a flash, my mam replied sarcastically, 'Toad in the Hole followed by Tapioca pudding!'

Mother's Ruin

. . .

Benny Dawson, a convicted drug dealer newly released from prison, moved into the Cranhill area of Glasgow to stay with his mother.

Within a very short time he was back into his old ways and making his presence felt in the local drug trade.

Whatever the drug he'd get you it, and he didn't care about who or how old his clients were. Making money fast was his focus.

His mother would also get involved by taking messages for him.

This did not go down well with Willie Cole, the local beat man who had built up a good relationship with the families of the community and engaged himself in several youth projects within the area.

Willie made a point of seeking out Benny Dawson and strenuously made him aware that he would not tolerate any drug dealing in his area and suggested he move out.

This ultimatum did not sit well with Benny and their meeting broke up with some angry words being exchanged.

A few days later Willie began receiving information regarding Benny and his continued drug deals and decided it was time to take action.

Firstly, he called at his home address and issued him with the Willie Cole drug dealers warning. That was – if Willie received one more call to the office or tip-off that Benny was dealing he would exact his own summary justice on him!

Several weeks and numerous complaints later, Willie saw Benny walking along the roadway toward him and when alongside he grabbed Benny by the arm and promptly apprehended him.

'You cannae dae me like that. I've got fuck all drugs on me!'

However, Willie just smiled at him and charged him with a breach of the peace, detaining him in custody for the court.

Less than a week later, Willie saw Benny again and promptly arrested him like before.

'Aw come tae fuck, Cole man, you're out of order,' protested an irate Benny.

'Well move away and I won't bother ye, but if you persist in staying in my area and dealing drugs, I'm jailing you every time I see you. Now do you get my drift, fuck-face?' replied Willie, as he pursued his promise to physically and verbally abuse Benny.

Benny for his part would retaliate with his own brand of verbal abuse. 'You'll move away before me, Cole man. This is my area and I'm staying put wi' my wee maw – she's settled here and so am I, so you can get tae fuck, I'm not for moving.'

After this last encounter, Benny tried unsuccessfully to keep a low profile, but the lure of the big bucks being made from his drug deals brought him to the forefront again.

As Willie was being driven down the road one evening in a police panda he caught a glimpse of Benny in a carry-out kebab shop and quickly signalled the driver to stop.

Willie alighted from the panda and ran into the shop after him.

'What has he ordered?' he asked the assistant. 'Never mind, whit ever it was, just cancel it 'cause he's coming with me!'

'Get you tae fuck, ye cannae dae this tae me!' he protested vigorously. 'You're totally out of order, but I'll tell ye what! Am no' movin', so gerrit up ye, Cole man!'

But Willie would just smile at Benny and say, 'Watch me!' As he frogmarched him out of the shop on his way to another custody lesson in Willie Cole's personal summary justice.

Complaints were made verbally by Benny to the duty officer, but he would never follow them through, and his threats toward Willie became more regular and more aggressive.

Still Benny refused to move away from the area and still he continued to be involved with supplying drugs to the area.

Try as hard as he might, Willie could never catch Benny with drugs in his possession, although he did arrest several of his runners, who dealt to feed their own habit. But their loyalty to Benny, coupled with their fear of retribution, would never allow them to provide the evidence required to arrest Benny for the possession and supplying of drugs.

More extreme measures were required by Willie, so he restructured his summary justice methods.

Benny had a visible weakness like an open wound and Willie decided it was time to throw the final dice.

Up he went to Benny's house and knocked on the front door. Moments later it was opened by his mother.

'Benny's not in so, if you don't mind, don't come back to my door, I don't want my neighbours upset,' she said rather cockily.

'I'm not here for Benny, Mrs Dawson, I'm here for you!' At that Willie took hold of her arm and led her, struggling, over to the police car waiting outside.

Benny was furious when he heard what Willie had done and arrived at the police office almost at the same time as his mother.

After a verbal exchange with Willie, Benny was informed in no uncertain terms, that this was how it would continue for the foreseeable future, until he moved away from the area.

Within a week of this incident Benny disappeared, although for several months thereafter Willie received anonymous death threats to his home!

Alex Gave him the Boot

• • •

Out on mobile patrol one day in an unmarked Jaguar with Alex Urquart, I was conscious of him becoming very agitated and annoyed by a driver in his rear-view mirror who had followed us all the way along the Great Western Road.

He was driving a few feet off the rear of our police car and certainly too close for comfort.

As Alex pulled up to stop at the automatic traffic signals, he put his police whistle in his mouth, jumped out the car, in uniform, went to the rear and opened our car boot and, drawing the attention of the driver with his police whistle, he signalled him to drive his car inside!

The driver, realising it had been the police he was tail gaiting, put his hand up apologetically, turned off the main road and disappeared down a side street.

Rock On

. . .

Some of the more light-hearted and pleasurable duties I had to serve during my time in the police force came when I was involved in escorting so-called celebrities, although some of them were so in love with themselves I'm surprised they ever noticed anyone else around.

Such was the case with one pop star celebrity. 'Hold me close don't let me go'! Don't think so.

I had to go to the Radio Clyde Station at Anderson in Glasgow, where the pop star was being interviewed by one Richard Park.

How they managed to fit both monster egos into one studio is a mystery we'll certainly never solve.

Apparently a crowd of girl fans had gathered outside the station (about twelve!) and his management feared a wild frenzy outside when it came time for him to leave.

So they notified photographers!

While waiting in reception, I met a young girl who had been sent over to the Clyde offices with a dispatch from her work and had been given permission by her boss to wait there in the hope she would meet the pop star and possibly have her recent purchase of his latest LP autographed.

After a long wait, this wee greasy looking gadgy character with French-combed hair and a hooped earring in his left ear eventually appeared with his entourage of a personal manager, a flunky and two gorillas.

As he walked out into the small reception area the young girl fan stepped forward with her LP.

Quick as a flash these two gorillas stepped forward, coming between her and the star and putting their hands out to hold her back.

So I intervened and said, 'This girl has been waiting for hours to meet you. She was also at your concert last night!'

He then stopped and turned toward her.

I thought to myself, 'Good one, Harry, she's going to get a wee peck on the cheek and an autograph.' How wrong I was!

'Did you enjoy it?' he asked her, while masked by his two gorillas.

'Yes! It was excellent thank you,' she replied politely.

'That's good,' he said as he turned away from her and walked out the door.

As the girl made to follow one of the gorillas placed his arm across her chest and, stopping her, he said, 'Now that's far enough, dear. Let's not get carried away.'

What an absolute big diddy this guy was, but I presume he was following orders. Nonetheless, this was totally uncalled-for behaviour.

Therefore, I decided that if he can't show good manners to her then I wasn't going to be helpful to him.

His management wanted to create a diversion, allowing me to take their star out of a side door to a waiting police vehicle and whisk him away. We would then meet up later and change over.

'Sorry!' I said. 'We are not allowed to use our police vehicles for that purpose!'

With me being stubborn and not allowing them any other alternative, the pop star had to leave by the rear door, where the twelve or fourteen girl fans were waiting who immediately besieged him, grabbing at his clothing and pulling out strands of his bouffant hair.

As someone who has been gradually losing his own hair over the years, it gives me no great pleasure accepting some responsibility that night for contributing to his rapid hair loss.

Lardy Spice

...

This is one of the most rotten things that I ever did during my police service and I now feel deeply embarrassed about it.

Joe Logan and I were in charge of the production department of the division when Joe received a call from the boss informing us that we were getting another member of staff.

A policewoman was returning from a long-term illness/injury and was on 'protected duty' so she was being seconded to our department for a few weeks.

The day she arrived: 'Shockeroony!' She hadn't wasted any time while she was off. I think she must have eaten half of Glasgow – she was humongous.

I reckon she was about 5'5" in height and 6'5" around her waist. Her arse was enormous! Hence the nickname, 'Lardy Spice Girl'.

It wasn't long before we realised why she had a weight problem. Firstly she ate everything and anything in sight and secondly, she was totally heart lazy and did bugger-all work.

Joe and I used to take certain seats and leave her with the tight one with arm rests. Well, it was tight for her.

We'd then ask her to assist us with something on one of the rows of shelves, as we peered over them, watching her trying to get up out of her chair without the chair getting jammed to her arse.

But worst of all was when we went to the baker's. We would buy two plain buns and one large cream-filled chocolate éclair. We would lay them down on the desk, make a cup of tea, move out the way and shout for her to help herself, while we watched.

She couldn't resist it and would plump for the big cream one and proceed to stuff it into her gub before we returned.

Tadpoles in the Bath
• • •

One of my father's many jobs was as a chimney sweep in our large housing scheme.

Every Saturday morning he would be off around his customers with his trusty old-fashioned ball and brush, a bag of old bed sheets and blankets to collect the soot and his trusty packet of sulphur to help detect what chimney he was sweeping.

He would run along the rooftops unaided and without a safety net, like the star attraction in a circus high-wire act!

At the end of the day, he would arrive home looking like one half of the minstrels, so it was my mother's job to run a hot bath for him and his dirty money.

After he had washed himself and his money and vacated the hot bath, it was a case of 'Don't waste the water!' so my younger brother Hughie and I would be sent in to use it up.

It was several years later that I was to discover what all the small, slimy black things with trailing tails were that floated about our bath.

Apparently my father cleaned chimneys for a living and afterwards, in the bath, he did likewise to every orifice on his face. Poor Hughie – for years I had him believing they were black tadpoles and he kept them in a glass bowl, hoping that one day they would develop into something.

It's no wonder they never hatched into frogs.

Lock Up Yer Sick

. . .

After a tiring back-shift, I was invited through to the back of the office for a farewell drink, courtesy of a member of the shift who was transferring to another specialist department.

We all sat around the table swapping stories and jokes while the alcohol flowed, until eventually it dried up and my partner Stevie, who was driving, informed me it was time for us to go.

As Stevie dropped me off at my house, we arranged that he would also pick me up the following day for our shift.

The following morning I awoke with the worst hangover and for the next few hours it didn't ease up. I felt as though I needed to be sick to be rid of this horrible feeling.

As time wore on, I got ready for my work and was duly picked up by Stevie.

All the way down the road, with the heat in the car coupled with Stevie's driving, I could feel my insides moving upwards towards my mouth and it was taking me a great deal of effort to hold them back, constantly swallowing.

Finally, we arrived outside the office and, as Stevie was preparing to reverse into a parking space, I opened the car door and jumped out.

I totally ignored Stevie's shouts and literally barged through the office front doors.

On seeing me, the bar officer buzzed the security door allowing me to enter, closely pursued by Stevie calling my name. Fortunately, the door closed before he reached it, thereby providing me with all the time I needed.

As I entered the corridor leading to the rear office, which was lined with an overspill of clothes lockers, I succumbed to the pressure of my insides wishing to appear on the outside of my body.

I grabbed the handle of one of the first locker doors I came to and fortunately for me it opened immediately, coinciding with me performing a male interpretation of Linda Blair's jet of vomit scene in the film *The Exorcist*! Huey, Ralf and Ruth all there.

'Harry, wait up there. What's yer hurry?' Stevie called out as he entered the corridor, concerned by my sudden departure.

I quickly closed the locker door over and wiped my mouth, all in the same movement, before answering him.

'My hurry? You know me, Stevie, just desperate to get started,' I said, instantly recovering some much-needed colour to my features.

I then began my shift with a soothing mug of tea and, as time went on, I returned to my old self again, having relieved myself completely of the cause of my nausea.

During my refreshment break, I took a wander down the corridor lined with lockers and, making sure there was no one around, I opened up the sick locker.

Blow me down, I had only just spewed my insides all over some poor unsuspecting bugger's black shoes and good uniform, which had been neatly folded and hanging in the locker.

I closed it over before any of it spilled out onto the corridor floor.

As I paced up and down the corridor, pondering my next move, I was beginning to feel very guilty about my actions, so I returned to the locker to have another look, when all of a sudden I was struck with a mighty feeling of relief. It was like a weight being lifted off my shoulders.

It was a traffic warden's uniform locker!

Now this might sound sick, pardon the pun, but it actually blended in with the yellow bands on the uniform!

Mistaken Identity
· · ·

I was contacted by the SNP and booked to perform with my band at a special fundraising concert in their Kilmarnock constituency.

We duly arrived and performed the gig, which proved to be a good night for all in attendance.

A few weeks later, I received a letter from the SNP leader, Alex Salmond, thanking us for our performance on the night and telling me to contact their entertainment manager, Peter Wishart, with regards to providing the musical entertainment for any future fundraising concert engagements.

I contacted Peter Wishart by telephone and explained that I had been informed by Mr Salmond to contact him.

During our conversation, Peter complimented me on our popularity and the publicity we had received for our recent Russian tour of concerts.

I thanked him sincerely for his comments.

Then, like a throwaway line, he remarked, 'It's a country that we have never performed in, although we have played almost everywhere else in Europe.'

'Oh! So you play in a band then, Peter?'

'Yes, I do!' he replied rather modestly.

'So! What's the name of your band then?' I asked him in all innocence.

To which he casually replied, 'RUNRIG!!'

Viagra

...

Eddie was an older policeman, who had been widowed for several years and was preparing to go out on a date with a single mother who had a teenage daughter.

He was discussing with me the prospect of a deep and meaningful romance forming between them.

Neither had had any sexual experiences with the opposite sex for quite some time but, convinced that this was about to be the moment, he asked me for some advice, 'just as a precautionary measure,' he said, of course.

'Buy a packet of condoms if you're that worried!' I suggested.

'No! No! No! Harry. I mean should I require it in the arousal stages! You know? To maintain an erection,' he said, as he nodded his head and winked his eye.

I recommended he pay a visit to his GP and explain his predicament to him.

A few days later I met up with him again and he gave me the thumbs-up.

'The doctor prescribed me Viagra. I can't wait to try it out! I've to take one about half an hour before I do anything!'

He was a happy man, totally revitalised by this prescribed sexual aid from his GP, who was totally understanding of his plight.

When the weekend arrived the entire shift went happily off on our separate ways to enjoy our well-earned break, but no one was happier than Eddie as he looked forward to his heavy date!

The Saturday night came and went and the following morning I was driving down the road when I saw Eddie leaning against the wall of the newsagent's.

He had what appeared to be a dose of the shakes and looked slightly unwell!

I parked my car and went over to him and said, 'Eddie! You okay? How did your night of sexual passion go?'

He looked at me with staring eyes, 'Fourteen times! Fourteen bloody times!' he blurted out boastfully.

'Fourteen times!' I repeated in total astonishment. 'Crikey, Eddie. You're lucky you never broke yer neck.'

At which Eddie replied, 'Broke my neck! I nearly broke my wrist – she never turned up!'

'Soap Powder'
· · ·
From *The Adventures of Harry the Polis*

(Archie and Spook are in the front office, discussing the new modern police issue Uniform and how to clean it.)

SPOOK: How is you sapposed to clean dem der new uniform trousers and tops?

HARRY: Have you tried the new soap powder?

SPOOK: As tried dem all man: As used Persil, Daz, Bold. Man, you just name it, As tried it!

HARRY: Well apparently the clothing stores have a special new issue!

SPOOK: What's it called den man?

HARRY: FUGG!

SPOOK: FUGG? As don't believe you!

HARRY: I'm serious! Apparently, if Persil doesn't work and Daz doesn't work then FUGG it!'

The Scottish Battle-Cry

· · ·

I have many stories to tell about touring with a Scottish folk band that I used to manage and perform with and this is another, about the time we courted disaster during a performance.

We were touring Moscow and decided to spice up the opening introduction, with a show of 'Check out how fit we are for our ages!', aimed at our many young student fans.

It was agreed while carrying out our pre-sound check prior to the start of the concert that we would arrange our large sound monitors in a position far enough from the front of the stage to enable us to come on from the rear.

When we made our entrance, three of the band members would then run forward and jump up and over the monitors, whereby they would land at the very front of the stage to acknowledge the introductory applause. Very athletic indeed!

Unbeknown to us however, during our absence after the sound check when were rushed off for our evening meal and then to prepare for the concert, the Russian stage crew decided to move the monitors further forward on the stage while making a last minute tidy up of the wires.

Now, totally unaware of these changes, we arrived back at the venue and on the introduction of the band, we entered the stage from the rear as planned.

As previously rehearsed during the sound check three of the band, now wearing Scottish tartan kilts commando-style, ran forward, completely blinded by the powerful lights which hadn't been illuminated earlier during practice, and failed to notice the monitors had been moved as they jumped higher and higher straight up and clear over the sound monitors like National Hunt jump jockeys!

Unfortunately for them they also jumped clean over the front of the stage.

It was like a scene from Beechers Brook at the Grand National, as together, as one, they all landed with a '*thud*!' in the front-of-stage orchestra pit!

Fortunately none of them were injured, although they did suffer from slight shock and embarrassment, but, like true wee Scottish braveheart soldiers, they carried on as if it was part of the stage act.

Afterwards, as our young Russian fans and a few remaining reporters gathered around for interviews and autographs we were asked to explain.

'What was the cry you all shouted out as you jumped off stage? Was it a Scottish battle cry you roared?'

We said yes it was, just to sound macho to our young friends, but it was really that old famous battle cry of the unexpected: 'Ohhhh Shitttttt!'

However, one daily newspaper reporter had somehow managed to get an explicit photograph of the action for his festival story.

Roughly translated, it said, 'What do real Scotsmen wear under their kilts? . . . Niet!' Accompanied by a photograph of three big pairs of danglies!

I must say, the publicity we received didn't do us any harm, and was welcomed by the festival organisers it also resulted in performing to sell out crowds for the rest of the tour.

No doubt all wanting to see us in the flesh, so to speak!

Speak to Me!

. . .

From *The Adventures of Harry the Polis*

(Harry and Spook are in the front of the Police Office and Spook is relating to Harry the story of his night out.)

SPOOK: So, I'm standing in de pub and I'm chatting up dis gorgeous blonde female.

HARRY: And?

SPOOK: Well! I'm hitting her with my best patter and I'm rapping some of my favourite Bob Marley lyrics, 'No woman no cry', and she's nodding her head and smiling dat me. She is dust lovin' dit man!

HARRY: Sounds to good to be true, but carry on, let's hear it.

SPOOK: She is smiling dat me, putting her head to de side and generally loving de crack. I thought to maself, Spooky my boy, you has de S.E.X. appeal!

HARRY: Oh hurry up! What happened?

SPOOK: Well! De next thing is, her girlfriend comes over to me an' says, I hope you can speak de sign language man, because Dana is a deaf mute!

Which reminds of the deaf and dumb Welsh coal-miner who got trapped down a coal shaft and broke four of his fingers shouting for help!

How the Mighty Fall

...

Over the years working a particular area you see the up-and-coming local hard man growing up and beginning to emerge as feared figures amongst the other neds.

This was the case over a short period of time with Johnny Jackson – 6' 3" in height and with a build manufactured in the local council sport centre.

Johnny was soon employed for his fear factor, starting out as a bouncer, or steward as they are now referred to, and progressing up the ladder to that of the enforcer for the area.

I remember receiving a call to attend at his home address with regards to a complaint of a domestic disturbance.

The young cop who I was partnered off with knew Johnny's background and reputation and displayed a slight hesitancy.

'Don't worry son, we have 7,000 members in our gang!' I said reassuringly.

Having had dealings with him recently on another matter, I found him to be fairly easy to deal with if the situation was kept calm.

On arriving at his apartment for the complaint, I learned very quickly that the disturbance was between him and his common-law wife.

I took Johnny to one side and spoke with him in private, man-to-man, pointing out the upset he was causing to his young daughter and his wife.

She didn't want him to stay while he was in this mood and I suggested it was better for all parties concerned if he left and stayed at his brother's house for the night, returning in the morning, when everybody had had a good night's sleep and was more relaxed and willing to talk it over.

Without any resistance Johnny readily agreed to my suggestion and left by taxi for his brother's house.

Not long after this incident, I was transferred out the area to another department and didn't have any other dealings with him.

However, within the next few years, I learned that Johnny had furthered his career and was not only the local enforcer and the most feared person in the area but had also become involved in the drug cartel and assumed the reputation of the main drug dealer for the area.

Soon he was driving around in a brand new BMW car and his wife was comfortable in her Cherokee four-wheel drive Jeep.

Johnny had also moved his family into a large detached house in a plush area; a luxury house befitting his new found wealth. Fancy, expensive holidays were only a telephone call away.

In a very short time, the up-and-coming Johnny had become the top dog! Well, he thought he was, with all this control, power, fearful reputation and wealth.

It poses the question, why then would he want to go up onto the roof of a high rise flat, stab himself with a large knife six or seven times, before throwing himself off the roof and committing suicide?

Apparently, there were no suspicious circumstances. Aye, right!

Could he possibly have got in too deep?

Or, maybe, just maybe, he awoke one morning with a very guilty conscience!

Freddie Starr was Nowhere

. . .

This story was related to me at a recent police officer's retiral doo by a colleague who threatened to buy me several large whiskies if I would include it.

He didn't have to threaten me, because I just loved it!

Two cops attend a complaint regarding a disturbance being caused by an ex-boyfriend within a house in Govan.

The female complainer had five children who resided with her in a large house with a long lobby entrance.

While speaking with her at one end of the lobby, one of the cops felt something hit his ankle and, on looking down, he saw a colourful ball.

Thinking that one of the children of the complainer had kicked it at him, the cop showed his technical football skills by flicking the ball up like Ronaldinho and volleying it, kicking it the full length of the lobby.

Pleased by his show of skills, he turned around to see a horrified look on the complainer's face, followed by screams of, 'Arrghh! The wean's wee hamster!'

This outcry suggested that something was deeply wrong.

The complainer ran the length of the lobby, picked up the ball and opening it up, she removed an unconscious pet hamster and immediately began to resuscitate the poor wee creature.

Fortunately, Jinky, the wee hamster, survived his ordeal and recovered in time for his next kick about!

Down Under

. . .

An idea to get more police officers out of the office jobs and back onto the street was to hold a series of interviews and employ qualified civilian station assistants capable of performing the duties presently occupied by a uniformed officer – that of dealing with the public and their complaints.

Graham became one of the first successful candidates and took up his duties immediately.

For the first few weeks Graham shadowed the outgoing police officer and was shown the various duties expected of him, and by all accounts he settled in well, displaying an eagerness to fully understand the duties of a force station assistant.

Within a very short time, having shown great commitment and learning abilities, Graham had assumed full responsibilities for the running of the office, supervised only by a uniform sergeant.

He also proved a hit with all the police colleagues on his shift and would regularly join in with the organised nights out.

Hence the news of his arrest and subsequent detention in custody was to prove a bolt out of the blue to everyone who knew him.

It appears our Graham was arrested along with an older male, who was wearing handcuffs, when the police attended a call regarding two men acting suspiciously at the rear of a housing tenement building.

The older male was identified as an Australian working as an airline pilot who was in Glasgow on a two-day stopover.

Graham had apparently met up with him in a gay bar within the city centre and they decided to get it on.

It was a complete shock to his police colleagues at the station for Graham had never displayed anything to indicate his sexual preferences.

In the absence of a station assistant, I was detailed the duties of bar officer to cover for Graham.

I was involved in the front office when the sub-divisional officer entered the station.

As he collected his daily despatches, he looked around the office and, focussing on me sitting at the duty officer's desk, asked, 'Where's Graham?'

Without any hesitation I replied rather casually, 'Oh Graham won't be in today. He's sharing a pair of handcuffs with an Australian pilot in a prison van en route to the sheriff court!' I then added, 'I wonder if it's the same pair!'

The sub-officer hesitated for a moment, digesting my reply.

'I beg your pardon?' he said.

'I was just wondering if it's the same pair of handcuffs they used on them!' I replied.

The sub-officer still hadn't grasped what I had said. 'Run that by me again,' he said.

To which I replied with a straight face, 'Graham was arrested last night along with an Australian aeroplane pilot, at the rear of a tenement close. Allegedly, our Graham was "down under" checking out the pilot's "undercarriage" and lubricating his "joystick" while down there! Allegedly of course!'

The sub-officer stood there stunned by this news and the graphic way I related it. 'Are you at the wind-up, Harry?' he asked in disbelief.

'No!' I replied. 'He was definitely an Aussie!'

'But it was Graham they arrested?' he asked concerned.

I nodded my head in reply to his question.

'Fuck me! You never know the minute,' he said, totally out of character, as he stood there pondering over the breaking news.

He then added, 'I personally interviewed him and he came across as an excellent candidate for the job, so much so that I recommended him. He certainly never gave the impression that he was a . . . '

As he hesitated, searching for the right word to describe Graham in a world ruled by political correctness, I interrupted him. 'I think the word you're looking for is, "mattress muncher" or maybe "pillow biter", if you get my drift.'

As he shook his head in amazement at Graham's predicament, he was about to enter his office, when I couldn't resist it: 'By the way, boss! Just for the record, when you say you personally interviewed him for the job . . . ' I paused for a moment.

'Yes! What are you going to ask, Mr Morris?' he said.

'Well!' I continued. 'Was he sitting across the desk from you – or was he under it?'

He allowed a wry smile to appear on his face before he closed his office door over.

Dining with Doctor Hook!
. . .

Having helped my colleague David Arnott and his wife Sylvia to move house, it was no surprised when I received an invitation to his housewarming party.

O'Reilly and big Ronnie made arrangements to pick me up so that we would all arrive together, stopping off for a few beers beforehand just to get us in the mood.

When we eventually arrived, the party was in full swing and we were the last of the invites to appear.

We quickly moved amongst the guests, mingling with some of his new neighbours and family relatives and in-laws.

Several drinks later, the music was getting monotonous, with Barry Manilow's vocals blasting out of the stereo system non-stop since we had arrived, so I decided it was time for a change.

I sidled over and at the end of the song he was singing, I quickly changed it over for the Bee Gees and *Night Fever*.

However, within a few minutes, it was *Tragedy*, as the DJ for the night reinstated Barry to the turntable.

Over on the left-hand side of the room and attracting a lot of attention, was a colourful fish tank, occupied by several brightly coloured goldfish.

'See that one with the black eye? We call it Doctor Hook,' said David. 'That's my daughter's favourite one.'

Later on in the evening, having heard this, I went into the kitchen and checked the cupboards for some carrots. On finding one, I sliced it up into thin cuts and, joining the main party again, I put my hand into the tank while holding onto a piece of carrot and, taking it out, I shook it about like a fish wriggling.

'They're slippery little buggers aren't they?' I said, as I

dropped it into my mouth, prompting some spontaneous laughter from the assembled party guests.

I then returned to the kitchen area, where O'Reilly and big Ronnie were pouring the drinks.

As we stood there talking we were joined by a wee, drunken neighbour of David's.

'Did you really eat that fish in there?' he asked me, while trying to focus his 'pontoon eyes' on me (one was happy and the other had gone for a twist!).

'Of course I did, you saw me!' I replied.

After a few minutes he began to annoy us and started spouting out the usual pish from a drunk.

'You're no' very big for a polis!'

'That's because I only deal with all the wee cases, but I don't need to be big, because I've got big Ronnie there,' I said.

He looked over at Ronnie and said sarcastically, 'Huh!'

That was the cue for Ronnie to grab him, put his arm up his back and lift him off the floor. Just short of breaking his arm, I persuaded Ronnie to drop him.

Picking himself up off the floor, he promptly left the kitchen for the sanctuary of his wife in the front lounge.

After several more drinks, we all returned to the lounge, where Barry was still on the turntable, singing about Lola, who apparently was a showgirl and having a much better time than we were at this moment in time, with a Puerto Rican called Rico, who wore a diamond, up until some jealous bastard called Tony arrived on the scene, then a gun went off, but who shot who is a mystery. All very confusing for the polis no doubt!

Anyways, enough was enough and so we ordered up a fast black to come to our rescue prior to slashing our wrists during the next Barry Manilow track, *Can't Smile Without You*!

I was dropped off first at my house and my head barely touched the pillow before I was fast asleep.

Early next morning, I was awakened with the telephone ringing.

'Hello!' I answered, barely awake.

The voice on the other side bellowed out over the phone.

'You rotten bastard, Harry Morris! You ate Doctor Hook.'

'Who the hell is Doctor Hook?' I asked him.

'It's the wean's favourite goldfish, it had a black eye like an eye patch. I cannae believe you did that and don't act as if you didn't, everybody at the party saw you.'

'It was a slice of carrot I ate, I was only joking.' I pleaded my case. 'I wiggled it about in the tank water as if it was moving, then I ate it.'

'Well Doctor Hook is missing and my wee lassie's heart is breaking,' he said, before continuing, 'Sylvia's mother said she saw you as well.'

'Sylvia's mother! What is this, the album charts?' I asked.

'Just don't deny it!' he screamed down the phone.

Not matter how much I pleaded my case, David wouldn't believe me. I even told him I would have eaten Barry Manilow's album before I'd have eaten Doctor Hook, but to no avail.

Needless to say, I never received another invite from David to attend any of his future parties.

By which time, having suffered a previous unfortunate experience with tropical fish in a showpiece aquarium at the police college, I was right off fish anyway!

Burns Supper Break

· · ·

A great favourite of mine in the police was the annual Burns Supper every January in memory of the Immortal Bard.

This particular year, I was a member of 'F' Division, so I decided to buy a ticket for theirs, which was being held within the Territorial Army halls at Woodgreen in Glasgow.

One of the colleagues on my shift and who was present at my table was Charlie Burns, no relation to the Bard, but a newly promoted Sergeant to the Division.

As with all Burns Suppers, the whisky, haggis and patter were flowing non-stop, particularly from the many humorous guest speakers who were booked to appear.

It was, as usual, a wonderful occasion for all who were in attendance and, like all good things, it drew to a close.

Nobody really noticed Charlie disappear but, as we all left, we naturally assumed his other half had arrived at the agreed time to pick him up and whisk him away.

We all assembled outside and were whittled down as our respective modes of transport arrived.

Surprise! Surprise! The following morning I learned that Charlie had broken both his ankles in an accident and was now occupying a bed in the local hospital.

It seems, unbeknownst to all of us at his table, that Charlie had gone to the toilet before leaving the hall but instead of going to the ground floor one he had somehow, in his drunken condition, gone upstairs to a toilet. During which time, he fell asleep.

When he eventually awakened, he found the door leading downstairs was locked. Unfortunately for him, the whisky he had consumed during the evening had blurred his vision and dented his brains and he forgot that he was upstairs. Assuming he was on the ground floor, Charlie decided to open a window and jump out onto the grass two or three metres below.

When he jumped out of the window he fell like a sack of potatoes ten metres onto the concrete path below sustaining his serious injuries.

As a result of this, poor Charlie lay there moaning in agony until he was discovered and subsequently assisted by a stranger out walking his dog who heard his cries for help and raised the alarm.

This was one Burns who wouldn't forget his first night out at a police Burns Supper on the 25th of January.

Time Zone

. . .

On the last nightshift of Keith Malcolm and Jimmy Clark, they were driving the patrol car in the early hours of the morning along a quiet deserted road leading to the motorway, when they stopped to comply with a red light.

As Keith checked the rear view mirror, he noticed a large articulated lorry approaching and stopping behind them.

When he looked in the rear view mirror again, the articulated lorry had disappeared, as had almost twenty-five minutes since they had stopped. What was going on? How come?

Case solved with a simple explanation: they had both fallen asleep!

Knock! Knock! Who is it?

. . .

A haulage contractor, whom I got to know well during my police service, was getting over the recent death of his father.

However, he wasn't exactly in mourning as his father had left the family home many years earlier and their relationship had become strained to say the least.

It was no surprise to me when I called in one day along with my partner for a casual cup of coffee and a chat that he should ask me what I was doing the rest of the day.

'We're going to Largs to note a statement from a possible witness in a case we are dealing with,' I replied.

'Will you do me a favour then, since it's a nice day,' he said sincerely, 'and take my faither with you for the run and just leave him on the beach down there?'

'Yeah! No problem, Geordie!' my young partner replied, thinking Geordie's father was present in the office.

At that, Geordie handed him a small wooden box.

'What's this then?' asked my partner.

Geordie replied, 'It's my faither! Or, should I say, his ashes!'

My young colleague was astounded at this lack of respect and pulled his hand away. But the best was yet to come, for Geordie had fitted a small toy doll's device inside that spoke a recording when activated by any vibration to the box.

Whilst sitting drinking our coffee, an elderly female arrived at the office to carry out some part-time typing and invoicing for him.

Geordie placed his small box of ashes on the desk beside her.

With the office door left open, I could hear him speaking with her and telling her what typing he required to be done.

He then came out the door of the office and said, 'Watch this, Harry!'

At that, he slammed the office door with slightly more force than was required.

This was followed seconds later by loud screams from the office secretary as she wrenched the door open and came rushing out like a bat out of hell and ran like the clappers up the middle of the road, narrowly avoiding oncoming traffic.

Geordie fell to his knees and burst into hysterical laughter at her spontaneous reaction.

'What was that all about?' enquired my surprised young colleague.

To which Geordie replied, 'This!'

He then knocked on the side of the box of ashes, activating the doll recording, which screeched, in a panicky voice, with added sound effects.

'*Knock! Knock! Knock!* Help! Help! Get me out of here!'

Ethnic Friends

• • •

Strathclyde Police conduct a strict policy and will not under any circumstances tolerate racism of any kind, and rightly so.

However, there are isolated occasions when the best intentions are meant but one slip of the tongue can land you in deep trouble.

One such occasion occurred several years ago, when I was out on the beat in the Pollokshields area of Glasgow with a brand new police probationer.

We received a call over our police radio, requesting us to attend a tenement building, to verify the home address of an Anwar Singh and inform his parents of his arrest for shoplifting in the city centre.

After verifying his home address, the accused would be released and reported to the procurator fiscal.

On the way to the address given, I informed my young probationer that this was a very common task for us to perform.

As with all calls to tenement buildings, this was yet another house on the very top floor.

Completely out of breath, I knocked on the door, which was answered by several Asian children, who stared intensely at both of us standing there in our police uniforms.

Eventually, Mrs Singh appeared at the door and began to converse with us in her native Urdu and it was obvious that none of them could speak English very well, the Polis included!

For a short time there was some confusion, when suddenly, an Asian male appeared on the stairs behind us, dressed in a Glasgow Corporation bus driver's uniform.

'Is there a problem here, officer?' he asked.

'Yes!' I responded. 'Are you Mr Singh?'

He nodded, confirming that he was and I then asked if I could speak with him inside the house.

He agreed to my request and led me past his family into the front lounge, where I broke the news to him.

The father was distraught and burst out crying. 'You know, I have five daughters and four sons, they are all perfect in every way and very clever, but this boy and only this one boy, he gives me trouble and heartache. Why? Why? Why? I have tried everything, you know. Why? Why? Why?'

My young probationer stood listening intently to the father, feeling extremely sorry for him, when suddenly, for some reason known only to himself, he blurted out, 'So I take it, he's the black sheep of the family then?'

The father suddenly stopped his ranting and just looked directly at my young colleague.

At which point, I decided it was time to excuse ourselves and make a hasty retreat from the family home, followed by some choice words for my young probationer where I made him aware that not everything we dealt with in the police was black and white!

Itchy! The Sequel

· · ·

Walking around Marks and Spencer's store while shopping, I bumped into a former colleague of mine, pushing his shopping trolley.

I had nicknamed him 'the Itch' in my days in the police motorcycle section. You know the type! The one who would get right under your skin and irritate you.

'Oh hi, Harry. How are you doing?' he greeted me politely.

'I'm doing fine, Jack, what about yourself?' I replied.

'Can't complain!' he said. 'I'm working as a driver for the council. And what about you? I hear you're writing a book. What is that all about?'

'Two!' I replied. 'I've written two books. They're about all the funny things that happened in the police during the shift, you know the kind of things I mean!'

He then raised his eyebrows and rubbed his finger tips together in a motion and asked, 'Are you making a bit of dough from them?'

'It's not bread, it's books, but yes, I'm doing alright, Jack.'

He then moved closer to me and whispered, 'Am I in them?'

'How could I possibly write a book and not mention you Jack, you annoyed the fuck out of me and everybody else in the motorcycle section – I just couldn't possibly leave you out!'

He gave me a wry smile and asked, 'What did you write Harry, tell me what you wrote about me?'

'I wrote quite a few stories about you Jack!' I teased him.

'Tell me what you wrote, Harry, tell me!' he pleaded with me.

'If you want to know what I wrote about you, you'll have to buy the books, ya miserable wee bugger!'

At that point, a white-haired woman appeared in our shopping aisle. On seeing her, Jack blurted out in sheer excitement, 'Pauline! You'll never believe it – Harry's written a book on me!'

I just stared at him in disbelief, shook my head and said, 'Two, Jack! I've written two books!'

Think Once! Think Twice!! Think Bike!!!

. . .

There was a road safety lecture given by the road patrol inspector with regards to the latest campaign, 'Think Once, Think Twice, Think Motorcyclist', and the need for taking more caution while riding a police motorcycle on patrol.

This came following recent statistics suggesting that motorcyclists were more likely to be involved in serious road accidents than anyone else.

With the need for caution and awareness fresh in our minds we left the lecture room to take up our patrol duties.

First out the garage was Alan Burke and as he raced down the slip road to join the main road, he failed to see an oncoming double-decker bus and promptly collided with the side of it, causing extensive damage to his police motorcycle and receiving injuries.

On his return to police duties after a few weeks off recovering from his injuries, he had to smile when he walked into the motorcycle garage and saw the wall of his parking bay displaying a large sign, which read:

'Think Once! Think Twice!! Think Big Corporation Bus!!!

Is that Kung-Fu?

• • •

During the early 1980s while on patrol one night in the Glasgow Cross area, the divisional van crew were flagged down by a very distressed female who was bleeding profusely from a deep head wound.

The injured female intimated that she had been assaulted by her husband, who had attacked her with a hammer in the nearby family home.

After summoning medical help for the injured female the officers attended the house – top flat, as always – within a restored older tenement building in Bell Street and found the husband totally blootered with the drink.

The officers made him aware of why they were there and asked, 'Where is the hammer?'

'You mean the fooking hammer?' replied the husband.

'Don't get smart, Mr! Now where's the hammer?' they asked again.

'It's oot the fooking windae!' he answered while laughing.

The officers did not take too kindly to his attitude and said, 'You'll be going oot the fuckin' windae if you don't tell us where it is!'

They pressed him for more information, in the knowledge that his wife's condition was serious and she had now been admitted to the Intensive Care Unit of the hospital.

He was asked again about the whereabouts of the hammer.

'The fooking hammer is oot the fooking windae!'

He then made his way over to the window within the living room area, where he repeated, 'Oot this fooking windae!'

One of the officers walked over and opened the window for a look and, sure enough, there on the ledge he saw a metal claw hammer, which he recovered.

The husband was duly cautioned and charged with the serious assault of his wife and thereafter locked up and detained in custody for court.

As the officers were noting the hammer as a production in the production book within the police office, they noticed the manufacturer's label attached to the shaft of the hammer.

On checking the label, they found and entered the hammer make as per the label description:

'One Fu-King make hammer, Made in China'!

Battery Hens now
Battery Fish

· · ·

A well-known drug dealer nicknamed 'Papa Dee' and his family of two daughters and seven sons, who were also his physical enforcers, lived in the centre of a housing scheme, where they had purchased their family council house and proceeded to add on several extensions and conservatories – making it stand out amongst the similar houses of the area, which were considerably more basic in appearance.

The older sons in the family had also used their persuasive charms to convince some of their next-door neighbours to part with their houses to them in deals that saw the neighbours having to move out to allow them to move in.

Anytime I had dealings with the father, or had a particular reason to call at his fortress, he would regularly strut about in a pair of shorts and a string vest like the outrageous Rab C. Nesbitt character and displaying more jewellery around his neck than Mr T of *The A-Team* and, to crown it off, he wore several large gold bracelets on both wrists and about 14 sovereign rings on each hand.

He must have been a nightmare for the airport security.

It was obvious he had an infatuation for gold. Either that, or he was a paid up member of the 'Metal Mickey Club'!

Inside the house was just as bad and a definite reflection of him, with ridiculous tacky colour schemes and totally outrageous furnishing adorning the living area.

Taking up pride of place within the front lounge, was a six-feet tropical community aquarium with a variety of colourful specimens of unusual fish, all shapes and sizes, which he would take great satisfaction in informing you he had imported many of the inhabitants of from Singapore and Hong Kong.

These were his real babies and he spent a lot of his money and time on this expensive hobby.

One particular day, armed with a search warrant, we called at his house for the umpteenth time to look for drugs.

It was basically an annoyance tactic on our part to make him aware that we would continue to make these calls at random.

As we were about to enter, he sarcastically called out, 'Put the kettle on Lizzie and make the boys a cup o' tea. We don't want them going back tae their office without having got something from us!'

He then invited us inside, while he casually ushered his four-year-old granddaughter out of his door, towards her own house opposite.

'Go and get yer mammy while these friends of papas come in for a copper tea.'

The small granddaughter was dressed in a fur coat with a hood and was pushing a small doll in a pram.

'Wait a minute, sweetheart! Let me have a wee look at yer dolly,' said one of the team as he prepared to check out the contents of the pram.

'Oh, come tae fuck and leave the wean alane, ya low life! She's no' done anything tae deserve that sort o' treatment,' said Papa Dee. 'Away inside and dae yer search!'

But the cop was not dissuaded and moved some of the clothing and the doll to one side, revealing a bag containing white powder and two bars of cannabis, hidden under the blankets.

This prompted Papa Dee to fly into a rage of abuse.

'Away ya dirty bastard. You planted them there. Yer lower than a snake's belly, dayin' that tae a wean, ya scumbag!'

The cop then lifted them out, held them up and said, 'Smile for the home movie, Papa, we're videoing it all and you're under arrest!'

At that the door opposite opened and one of his scantily dressed, skinny daughters appeared.

'Whit's goin' on?' she enquired, before beckoning the little girl toward her and continuing, 'Whit's up, Papa, whit are they dayin' tae ye?'

'They planted some drugs in the wee yin's pram and their trying tae say their mine!'

Quick as a flash his daughter accepted the ownership of the drugs: 'They're mine! They're aw ma drugs, I put them in my wean's pram tae hide them. They're ma ain personal use!'

'Okay!' said the Boss. 'Jail her as well and get the two of them down the road right away, before anymore of his family appear to accept the blame!'

At that point, they were both whisked off immediately, prior to the arrival of several more of the family, who had been rudely awakened from their long lie in.

As we executed our search warrants for both house addresses, we discovered the youngest of the spotty-faced brothers, wanted on warrant, concealed behind the bath panel in the toilet.

'Let me guess pizza face – ye're a plumber?' I said sarcastically.

Like a finely tuned robot, his first words to me were, 'By the way, they were ma drugs ye found. I planked them last night when I came tae visit my sister!'

'Aye right!' I replied. 'Join the queue behind yer sister.'

As the search continued in Papa Dee's house, the boss asked for the use of my police Magnum torch.

Later on, when he returned it to me, he said, 'You need new batteries for your torch Harry, there's none in it.'

I took it back, surprised by this remark, but never gave it a second thought.

After we had completed a thorough search of both houses, we all left Papa Dee's house to return to the police office and submit our paperwork, with regards to our search and our subsequent apprehensions.

Several months later, I had occasion to attend at Papa Dee's home on another matter and was invited into the house.

While there, I couldn't help but notice that his showpiece tropical aquarium was clouded and lacking any of his prized fish, which were extremely noticeable on my last visit.

'What happened to your tank? Where are all your fish?' I asked him.

'They're aw deid! As if you didn't know!' he replied angrily.

'How would I know that?' I enquired, genuinely unaware of why he was alleging any involvement by the police.

'Oh I take it you're Mr Innocent and know fuck-all about the Duracell batteries that just happened to find their way into my aquarium when you were last here?

'Wiped oot aw my babies, but I know it wis yous bastards that did it, you're the only bastards who would dae such an evil act!'

I decided it was better to make a hasty retreat, as his mood was changing and he was becoming really upset by his extreme loss.

There was also the fact that I had now sussed out exactly what happened to my torch batteries on the day of our drug search!

Toilet Humour

• • •

From *The Adventures of Harry the Polis*

(Spook has an upset stomach and is talking to Harry about it.)

SPOOK: Gee man, as had such a dose of de runs, as seriously thought as was melting in there!

HARRY: You know what they say about the skitters! They run in your genes.

SPOOK: Very funny, man, but I got a problem here.

HARRY: Well Spook, there's two things you can do about it!

SPOOK: And what is they man?

HARRY: You can swallow a wee drop o' Bisto and thicken it up a bit!

SPOOK: Come on man. But be serious, what can I do about it?

HARRY: Simple! The next time you feel like a wee Greyfriars Bobby . . .

(Harry pauses.)

SPOOK: Well, man, c'mon tell me!

HARRY: Just don't bother yer arse!

Bring Out Yer Dead

• • •

Auld Boab MacDonald was the first cop I worked with when I started my police career.

A more grumpy and crabbit old bugger I've yet to meet, but a funny guy when he really wanted to be.

One dayshift, over a cup of coffee, auld Boab was telling me about a time when he was drinking on duty daily and it didn't matter what shift he was working either.

He had been taken aside by his supervisor and warned about his drinking on duty and smelling strongly of alcohol. Any more of it and he was to be disciplined.

Boab ignored the warnings and continued to frequent his old beat haunts, where he was being offered and supplied with alcohol.

One particular favourite haunt of Boab's was a certain Co-op funeral parlour on his beat. The undertaker, his assistants and Boab would regularly have a swally.

However, one particular night, supplied with information about this, the chief inspector, the shift inspector and sergeant were left with instructions from the divisional commander to catch him in the act and present him up for discipline proceedings.

That night, after Boab had left the office after his official refreshment period, he sauntered down the road on his way to the Co-op parlour.

On arrival, he knocked on the rear door and it was answered by one of the assistants, who welcomed Boab inside, closing the door behind him.

Unbeknownst to Boab, he had been followed down the road by the supervisors detailed to catch him out.

They waited for a short time, in order to allow Boab

sufficient time to have tasted one, perhaps two large whisky drams, before they set into motion their trap to catch Boab.

Firstly, the inspector would position himself at the front of the premises and the chief inspector and the sergeant would cover the exit from the rear doors.

Once in place, they would contact the radio controller to call up Boab's divisional number and request his position to meet the sergeant and, as he walked out of his doss, they would then get him for being off his beat and, more seriously, for drinking!

However, the controller, having overheard the duty officer talking about a sting, quickly deduced that Boab was the one they were out to capture red-handed as, being a senior cop on the shift, it would set an example to all the younger cops about the dangers of drinking on duty.

Meanwhile, Boab is oblivious to all that is happening outside and is sitting back with his tunic and hat lying over a coffin while enjoying a good old blether and a large whisky with his mates in the funeral parlour.

Suddenly, his radio bellowed out his divisional number, which Boab initially ignored. Then it bellowed it out again.

This time Boab answered it.

'Give your position for the Sergeant to rendezvous,' he was told.

Boab responded by giving a location further down the road, away from his present one.

He stood up from his seat, lifted his hat and tunic and said to his friends, 'I'll be back shortly once I get a sign in my notebook!'

Boab was making his way to the door when the phone

began ringing in the office and one of the assistants answered.

'Hold up there Boab! There's a Donald McAuley on the phone for you. He says it's urgent.'

Donald, (the controller) told him in no uncertain terms not to go outside – 'They're waiting for to catch you!'

Boab thanked Donald and replaced the phone.

The colour had drained from his face and he now feared the worst for his job, as they hatched such an elaborate plan to trap him.

'What's up Boab? You look like you've seen a ghost! D'you want a hauf afore ye go out?'

Well! That was definitely the last thing he needed!

Boab then explained who was waiting outside to catch him and it looked like curtains for his police career, because a chief inspector doesn't stay on after dark to do anything unless it's serious.

He resigned himself to having to walk outside and meet his fate.

'Hold on a minute, Boab!' said the undertaker. 'Are you saying that they're waiting for you tae walk outside so they can report ye for discipline?'

'Exactly!' Boab replied. 'They must have followed me down!'

'Well that's not a problem!' he said confidently. 'They're outside waiting for you tae walk oot, right? Well ye don't walk oot! Ye get carried oot!'

He then turned his head and focussed on an open coffin.

'Just pop yersel' in there and Billy and Albert will carry you outside, right past them, into the hearse, take ye doon the road a bit and drop you off. Simple!'

By this time, any whisky Boab had consumed was now

running freely down his legs, with the fear of being caught, disciplined and the end result.

'Spot on!' said Boab. 'They're hardly likely tae stop a hearse tae check oot the contents of a coffin. They'd be really sick if they did that!'

Convinced this was his only way out of the present situation, Boab climbed into the coffin and the lid was closed over.

Outside, the supervisors hovered like sharks awaiting some unsuspecting surfer to appear in the water.

The door at the rear of the funeral parlour opened and they readied themselves to pounce, when out walked the undertaker's assistant.

He calmly walked over in the knowledge he was being observed and casually opened the rear door to the hearse, before returning inside.

Moments later, the main rear door was opened and out came the assistants carrying a coffin, which they loaded into the hearse before closing the door and getting into the front.

All the time they were being observed by the supervisors.

As they drove off out the yard, the supervisors returned their focus to the door, awaiting Boab's appearance.

A few hundred yards down the road and out of view of the supervisors, the hearse stopped and the assistants slid the coffin out the back onto the footpath.

It was then opened to allow Boab to be resurrected, so to speak, back onto his beat.

Once outside, Boab confidently called the controller and asked for an estimated time of arrival for the sergeant at his location.

Donald couldn't believe Boab had managed to do a

Harry Houdini on the supervisors while being surrounded and took great satisfaction in broadcasting Boab's message.

Totally dumfounded and puzzled as to how Boab had got away, the chief inspector and inspector returned to the office, while the sergeant went on to meet with Boab at the rendezvous.

But . . .

I am reliably informed that Donald the controller, received several calls from confused members of the public, reporting that a funeral hearse had just emptied the contents of a coffin onto the footpath and the body had got out and walked off!

Now I ask you! Who is going to believe that?

Which reminds me of a small relevant saying: 'It isn't the cough that carries you off, It's the coffin they carry you off in!'

Well it certainly was in this case. Or should I say, 'casket'?

Which also reminds me, while reading the newspaper the other day, I saw that the man identified as 'Larry La Preece', famous for writing the lyrics to that well known dance hall favourite, the *Hokey Cokey*, died recently and seemingly his death caused real problems for the undertaker at the funeral parlour when trying to put him into his coffin.

Apparently, they put his left leg in, his left leg out, in, out and they shook it all about . . .

Danny Boy!

• • •

A story I've told many times as a guest speaker is about the time my son Scott did a stint in a funeral parlour as work experience.

All day he worked with the undertaker, stripping each body of clothes, washing it down on both sides and drying and covering it in a clean white sheet, before sliding it away in a large drawer.

There was one more body left to perform this procedure on and the undertaker asked Scott, 'Do you think you could handle doing this body yourself? 'Cause I have a ticket for a Rolling Stone concert at the SECC – I've waited a year for this and need to get going or I'll be late.'

'Not a problem,' replied a confident Scott. 'I can do that. On you go, big man, I'll be just fine!'

Reassured by these words, the undertaker was off out the door, leaving his mobile phone number should any emergency arise.

Scott wheeled the last customer into the parlour and began the first task of stripping it of all clothes.

This done, he then washed down the front of the body and was turning it over to wash the back, when he saw a wine bottle cork, sticking out from it's bum!

He gently pulled the cork out and immediately it began to sing,

'Oh Danny Boy, the pipes the pipes are calling!'

He quickly replaced the cork.

He then had a good look all around the parlour, looking for some hidden camera, or a sign saying, 'You've Been Framed!!'

But nothing! Zilch!

He walked back over to the corpse and taking hold of the cork, he pulled it out of the bum again and just like before it began to sing,

'Oh Danny Boy, the pipes the pipes are calling!'

He quickly replaced the cork once more.

Completely baffled and unsure of what he should do, he called the undertaker on his mobile phone,

'You'll need to come back to the parlour, I've got a problem,' Scott informed him.

'What kind of problem?' asked the undertaker from his Rolling Stones concert.

'I can't explain it to you over the phone. You'll have to see it for yourself,' Scott said.

'Oh, alright!' he replied. I'll be right over.'

With that said, the undertaker left the concert, jumped into a fast black taxi and headed for the funeral parlour.

On his arrival, he got out and ran inside to check out the problem.

'What's up, Scott?' asked the undertaker.

'Watch this.' Scott then walked over to the corpse and as before, he removed the cork from its bum. It immediately burst into song,

'Oh Danny Boy, the pipes the pipes are calling. From glen to glen and –'

The undertaker interrupted and said rather angrily to Scott, 'You mean to tell me you got me to leave a Rolling Stoned concert just to hear an arsehole singing *Danny Boy*?!'

Not Quite Quincy

...

During my initial training after enrolling in the police the entire class of students had to attend the chief medical officer for all our required injections.

Not exactly an appointment we were relishing or looking forward too, but it had to be done.

As we queued up outside his room, there was no particular order we had to be in – it was just a case of line up and move forward when it was your turn.

I took my place in the line-up between big Robert Hagan and Eddie O'Reilly.

As we shuffled forward, Hagan, reaching the front, was summoned next and as the doctor turned around to face him with the hypodermic needle, big Hagan promptly collapsed in a heap, dropping to the floor like a sack of potatoes.

I turned to O'Reilly to say, 'Did you see that?' when 'Wallop!'

He promptly collapsed to the floor at my feet, followed by another student in the line behind him.

It was beginning to resemble the opening scene at the start to the popular television series at that time, *Quincy, ME*, and as I bent down to assist O'Reilly, the chief medical officer shouted, 'Just leave him lying and step forward for your inoculations!'

That was the thing that spooked me – that plural word, 'inoculations'. I could have quite easily have joined the others on the floor, as my arse collapsed with a sudden thrust of fear, but fortunately, I was able to pull myself together, step forward and receive my inoculations! Plural!

Billy Brown's Ear-Ache

• • •

Walking around my beat area one night with my young neighbour Zippy, we were approached by Billy Brown, a local ned.

'Hi, Zippy! How's it gaun?' he asked.

Now, if there is one thing I hate, it is a wee ned calling a police officer by his first name, never mind his nickname.

'Fine, Billy,' Zippy replied, as though he had to talk to him. 'By the way, Zippy, see that wanker Boaby Ferguson? The first chance I have, he's getting chibbed!'

As Zippy continued to talk to him, I stood several feet away and called up on the radio to check one William Brown for any apprehension warrants.

While I was doing this, Zippy was looking over towards me, having heard me calling for the check on Billy in his earpiece.

My luck was in as I received the following reply, 'We have an apprehension warrant outstanding for a William Brown of Pinkerton Avenue.'

I turned to Zippy and his 'friend' and said, 'Ho son! Where do you live?'

He looked at Zippy before answering, 'Pinkerton Avenue. How?'

I then radioed the controller, 'That's affirmative, can you please have the van rendezvous with me at the locus, regarding one male apprehension.'

Zippy continued to talk total tripe to this wanted ned until the van turned into the street, at which point I walked forward, took hold of his arm and placed my handcuffs on him while taking great satisfaction in informing him, 'Guess what sonny? You're wanted on warrant.'

He looked at Zippy and said, 'You're a fly bastard, Zippy, deliberately distracting me!'

'Don't think so sonny, I'm taking sole credit for this. Me! And only me,' I informed him.

Back at the office, I led him to the charge bar and the duty officer noted his details for his detention in custody.

During this procedure, he repeatedly turned to Zippy and openly threatened him.

'Next time you're in the Glen, ye're getting it!' he said.

'Lock this wee shite pot in a cell, Harry, and shut him up,' said the duty officer as he handed me the cell keys.

As I led him up the cell passage, I came to the cell allocated to Billy and put him inside, locking the door behind him.

At that point, a prisoner in a cell further along the passage called to me, asking for a drink of water.

I walked to the end where the sink was and filled his mug, and was returning with it, when the flap on Billy's cell door opened and he pushed his head through the space to look down the cell passage totally unaware of my presence behind him.

He then started to shout and mouth off, 'Zippy, ya prick! You and "Harry the bastard" are getting done!'

The words had barely left his mouth when I walked up to him from behind and gave him a gentle slap on the head.

'Hard Man' Billy received such a fright he pulled his head back in that quick he nearly ripped his ear off on the metal door flap.

Count Me In, Out!

• • •

I suffered a serious back injury on duty and it not only took me a long time to recover from it but it curtailed all my sporting activities.

However, it's usual on the police force to try to cover up your injuries and not to let anybody know that you are actually worse off than you are portraying outwardly!

Such was the case when one of the younger cops approached me in the knowledge that I had played football in the past and asked if I would like to make up the numbers in a friendly game of five-a-side football.

'Yeah, no problem,' I said confidently. 'Count me in anytime!' Thinking to myself that nearer the time I would cancel with some elaborate excuse, rather than just admit, 'I can't play anymore!'

'Good, you'll be in my team. We're playing tomorrow at two.'

I gulped, swallowed, farted then generally shit myself, as I certainly couldn't make an excuse up at such short notice that was good enough to allow me to cancel without looking bad.

That evening, I looked out my old sportswear kit and packed my bag for the following day.

After the shift, we all made our way to the sporting venue.

'I'll play in goals,' I offered, but after several had whizzed past me it became rather obvious that I was totally useless in goals.

So it was decided to change my position to play my old role as a defender.

I was the oldest in my team and the second oldest was

some 21 years my junior. I couldn't believe I had let myself get talked into this situation.

However, I bravely ran about like a teenager (well you know what I mean!).

At one point I thought I would be smart, when I noticed we had been playing for about one hour and twenty-five minutes.

'When is half time, guys?' I said rather smugly.

'We're just going to play for another five minutes, then call it a day,' replied Sidney, my team captain.

'Thank fuck!' I thought to myself, trying to remain upright.

The final whistle went and I immediately grabbed my sports bag.

'Where are you going, Harry?' I was asked. 'Are you not having a shower?'

'Shower!' I thought. 'It's connected to a heart monitor I want, along with a bottle of fuckin' oxygen and a big nurse to give me the kiss of life.'

But I casually answered, 'No! I'm just going to have one when I get up the road thanks.'

'What about a beer? We're all going for a drink,' he said.

'I'll need to miss out Sidney, I promised the kids I'd take them out on their bikes for a cycle.' What utter bullshit I was spouting out now!

'Oh well, thanks for coming along and I'll let you know when the next game is.'

'Yeah! Please do that. I'm up for it anytime,' I replied as I quickly rushed out the door to my car, prior to collapsing.

I got into my car and sat for a moment, while trying to regulate my heartbeat and my breathing, before I attempted to operate the pedals with my weak legs and blistered feet.

I slowly made my way up the road at 10 or 15 mph, eventually arriving at my house, where my back had now seized and I had to fall out my driver seat onto my path and crawl the last 10 metres to my front door.

Once inside, I immediately popped three of my prescribed DF 118 painkilling tablets and two Ibrufen 600s for starters, as I ran a hot Radox bath.

While doing this, I caught a glimpse of my face in the mirror – I resembled Berti the Beetroot Man.

The heat from my body was even steaming up the bathroom tiles.

I was so bad, that by the time I managed to get out of the bath, I had to go straight to bed, with my electric blanket on full.

It was only 4pm in the afternoon!

With the aid of my prescription drugs, I managed to sleep straight through until 6am the following morning, when my radio alarm went off.

Completely doped up to the hilt with medication, I ventured into my work and I genuinely don't remember how I got there.

A serious consideration was that I possibly flew with the amount of drugs I had taken for the pain!

I decided that I would stay in the office and catch up with some reports that were overdue. I certainly couldn't go out.

Later that day, Sidney came into the writing room and we were speaking, 'Are you not in pain today Harry? The rest of the guys are all a bit stiff and sore, Tam Rogers can hardly walk.'

'Not at all', I replied. 'Your problem is, you all need to do a bit of extra fitness training, particularly Trigger.'

Fortunately, he hadn't seen me after I had left him that day.

'We'll be organising another game next week if you're interested in playing again?' he said.

'Me, interested! Definitely, put me down first in your list,' I responded stupidly, while pressing down hard on one of my bollocks, in an act of self-hurt! Punishing myself for my macho man image and being unable to keep my big basterting mouth shut!

'Right then, I'll let you know,' he replied as he left the room.

Left alone in the writing room, I couldn't resist punching myself on the mouth twice and hitting my head off a locker three times!

Why couldn't I just shut the fuck up and maybe they would forget about me?

I continued to suffer in silence, fooling everyone into thinking I felt no pain and I was genuinely writing up reports, when Sidney, the sadistic wee bastard, re-entered the room.

'Harry! We're trying to arrange a game for the end of the week, how does that suit you?'

'Yeah! That's good for me, but let me know the exact day nearer the time.' I replied enthusiastically, like I really gave a flying fuck!

The rest of the week, was followed by the same ritual of me coming home at 2pm, hobbling up the driveway, slipping into a hot bath, crawling into my hot bed, topped up with strong painkillers and now coupled with morphine capsules, trying to sleep the pain away, until I had to get up at 6 a.m. the following morning, top myself up with medication and put on a brave face before arriving at work.

I would then walk in and cover up the severe pain I was suffering for the next seven hours, rather than let anyone know that I was totally unfit and hurting like hell.

Finally, the last day arrived before going off for my much needed rest days and I rushed out to my car for a quick getaway before 'Sid the Sadist' could catch sight of me.

Too bloody late! A cry rang out in the car park, 'Harry! Wait up there.'

I looked around and lo and behold, surprise, surprise, it was Sidney! How un-fuckin'-fortunate was I?

'You available tomorrow for a game of five-a-side?' he asked.

'Definitely, Sidney! You know me, I'm always up for it.' The words were out my mouth before I could stop myself!

At this point, I think my body is possessed and some masochistic, evil, hurtful bastard has it in for me and is deliberately moving my lips and talking. I just can't shut up!

'Great stuff! I'll see you at 2pm tomorrow then!'

At last I had control of my big gub and responded immediately.

'2 p.m.? Oh no,' sounding downbeat, 'not 2 p.m.! I can't Sidney, I've got to baby-sit the kids.'

'Oh that's a pity,' he said, sympathising with me.

Inwardly, I'm jumping up and down ecstatically and congratulating myself – 'Ya beauty! Thank you! Thank you! Thank you!'

I had managed to get myself out of having to play fives and save face at the same time, but disaster struck, as my big bloody mouth couldn't keep shut and blurted out loudly, 'Mind and keep me informed about any future games Sidney, you know I'm up for it!!'

My macho man act of stupidity resulted in me having to make three visits to the osteopath for treatment to my back, costing me a cool seventy-five pounds of my hard earned money.

Plus several months avoiding any physical activity!

And Sidney of course!!

Power From Above

• • •

There was a hold up on the Kingston Bridge flyover in Glasgow – the result of several vehicles being involved in a pile-up road accident – and several police motorcyclists were assigned to attend and deal with the situation promptly.

While it was being dealt with a blue Toyota car drove straight through a space in the congested traffic, the driver totally oblivious to what had occurred.

I mounted my motorcycle and gave chase after him and, as I rode alongside the driver's door, I stood up on my motorcycle and, controlling my bike with one hand, I banged on the roof of his car loudly with my other – *Bang*! *Bang*! *Bang*! – to draw his attention.

It turned out to be a priest who was daydreaming and received such a fright he immediately responded by looking upwards, searching the ceiling of his car for the cause of the noise.

To this day completely unaware of my presence, I think he suspected that Lord God Almighty was making a personal appearance for him in his Toyota motorcar!

Intermittent Faults

· · ·

The Wireless Workshop section of the police based at Helen Street in Glasgow employed excellent technicians but only one real character – his name, Robert Lester!

Robert, although a disabled person, was at the top of his field. He also possessed a nervous stammer, so that when he spoke it was like talking in instalments.

However, this did not deter Robert in any way. In fact it made him more of a personality in the section and he was known as someone who enjoyed a good laugh, even if it was at his expense.

One day I called at the workshops with my surveillance motorcycle and a transmitting fault with my radio.

I sought out Robert to check it out and, after a few jokes, which took him ages to tell me, he set about repairing my radio defect.

Within a very short time he had effected the repair and called up the force control room to give him a verdict on how good his signal was.

'W-wi-wire-wirelllesss W-wo-work . . . shops calling Fu-fu-force Cun-cun-controlll Roooom, hhow dddoo you you receive tthis ssignal, over?'

The force controller replied, 'Please note Wireless Workshops, that you have a very poor and intermittent signal. Suggest you try again!'

Robert turned to me and said, 'Tha-that's y-you!' He then added, 'D-d-don't llisten tooo tha that cu-cun-controller, th-th-the signal is pur-pur-perfect!'

Wee Jinky the Linesman

· · ·

I was saddened to learn of the sudden death of one of Football's greatest sporting talents, Jimmy Johnstone, a sad loss, following such great names as George Best and Jim Baxter.

You would have had to come from another planet if you had never heard of the name Jimmy 'Jinky' Johnstone.

Come to think of it, having seen him perform on the park, *he* was from another planet. Well, definitely out of this world!

Jimmy had forged out a very successful career with his beloved Glasgow Celtic Football Club and was to form part of the now famous Lisbon Lions, affectionately named after they won club football's top prize, the European Cup.

I met with and got to know Jinky about twenty years ago, after he had retired from playing football and was now working for a well-known builder's firm in Glasgow.

I would occasionally call in during my motorcycle patrol and enjoy a cup of tea with wee Jinky and some of the staff, during which Jinky was never slow to relate a funny football story.

In 1982, I was writing a magazine about the funny stories and situations I had encountered during my police duties, to be sold in order to raise money for a south-side orphanage within my patrol area.

I had secured stories from Sean Fallon, the assistant manager of Celtic FC and the Honourable David Hodge, former Lord Provost of Glasgow and mentioned the fact to Jinky.

'Okay, big man, I'll give ye a story for yer magazine,' he said, volunteering the following piece.

Getting into the Scotland international team proved to be a problem for him and there was two reasons for that.

Firstly, Willie Henderson of Glasgow Rangers, who was his good friend and biggest rival and who was currently holding down the right wing position.

Secondly, the international team was influenced by a clique of players who stuck together and did not take kindly to change!

However, following the injury and subsequent withdrawal of wee Willie, he was named in the pool with every chance of playing – his form was outstanding at that time, so they couldn't possibly overlook him.

Now the present international team manager was a part-time guy called Walter McCrae who also doubled as the manager of Kilmarnock Football Club.

The twenty-one international players selected for the pool gathered for training to prepare for the forthcoming midweek game, but nothing could have prepared Jinky for what was to come next.

Afterwards the coaching staff arranged for a 'bounce' practice match amongst the players.

The manager read out the list of players to take part in each practice team and, as there were ten on each side with one remaining, Mr McCrae handed Jinky a red flag and asked him to run the line!

Now! I don't need to go into the exact words Jinky used, but suffice to say, he informed Walter in very explicit terms where to stick his red flag.

As it was, the midweek international match came and went.

The following Saturday, with the international players having gone back to their respective teams, it was back to normal and a return to club football.

Glasgow Celtic, by sheer coincidence, just happened to be playing a Scottish League game away at Rugby Park against Kilmarnock Football Club, managed by the aforesaid Walter McCrae.

Jinky, for his part, was on a mission. He had a personal point to prove to the part-time Scotland international manager!

During the game, in which wee Jinky ran amok and tormented the Kilmarnock defence, he was voted the outstanding 'Man of the Match', having scored two goals and set up two other goals, in an impressive four-nil win for Celtic.

As the final whistle was blown by the match referee, wee Jinky made a beeline for the players' and officials' tunnel.

With perfect timing, Walter McCrae was getting out of the home team dugout and was just straightening up when wee Jinky ran past him and couldn't resist attracting his attention with the immortal words, 'Hey, Walter! Not bad for a linesman, eh?'

Not Exactly Earl Grey!

· · ·

Sadly, my partner's father has succumbed to that terrible heart-breaking disease, Alzheimer's!

As a fair, hard working supervisor he was held in high esteem by the many men who knew him and worked under him.

He also possessed a wicked, dry sense of humour that would still occasionally surface during a visit.

Recently, while attending at his nursing home, my partner was busily tidying up his room, after which she asked him, 'Would you like me to make you a cup of tea, Dad?'

'Oh aye!' replied Jim. 'That would be nice hen.'

She then walked over and lifted his silver-plated teapot from the side of his bed and said, 'Will I make it in your favourite silver teapot, dad, so we can all have a cup?'

'If you want tae hen, but I'd rather you didn't,' he replied.

'Why? What's wrong with it, dad?' she asked him.

'It tastes o' pish,' was the gruff reply.

'It's your favourite teapot! How could it taste like that dad?'

Too which Jim looked straight across the room at me and replied, with a wicked grin on his face, ''Cause I pee in it during the night, tae save me getting up to the toilet!'

Flaming Flumes
• • •

When my son Scott turned 10 years of age, for his birthday treat he asked for me to take him and four of his best friends along to the Time Capsule, a newly opened swimming resort fitted out with huge waterfalls, wave machines and twisting speed flumes.

As soon as we entered the doors, we made for the dressing rooms and quickly changed into our swimwear, with all the boys eagerly wanting to get to the flumes to experience the thrill of sliding down them in a race.

The rules were that all children of a certain age had to be accompanied by an adult. So along with the five boys I ascended the many, many steps leading to the rooftop of the building and the start of the flume tunnel.

Normally, I would have required several days to recover from such an enduring trek up stairs, but as it was I had to make do with several minutes in order to display a macho image for my son Scott and his excited young friends.

Having scaled the heights to the summit of the flumes it would not look very macho of me if I waited until they all went down the flume and then made my escape back down the stairs, passing everyone of all shapes and sizes on their way up to them.

'Come on, dad, you're allowed to do it as well!' said my son Scott, grinning like Damien from *The Omen*!

'Yeah, Mr Morris! My dad did it,' boasted one of his young brat disciples with a wicked streak for seeing grown men cringe!

'Why not?' I replied, totally unconvincingly, trying hard to persuade myself that it was probably a better prospect and a much quicker descent than having to face all those stairs again and, after all, it would make me look good in front of Scott and his friends.

'Okay then! On you go. I'll give you all a start and I'll see you all at the finish! Once I've overtaken you!' I said rather nonchalantly, unaware of the sadistic architectural design of this death wish obstacle awaiting me or the fact that I was about to re-enact the Arnold Schwarzenegger scene from the sci-fi film *The Running Man,* without the aid of any protective casing around me.

'Are you next, sir?' asked 'Morticia', the female pool assistant.

'Most definitely – I'm next,' I surprisingly replied like a total diddy, trying to appear calm and disguise the pounding noise emanating from my beating heart!

I took up my position on the high seat at the start and held onto the metal bar above waiting for the signal to go.

After a few moments the pool assistant said, 'Excuse me sir, but you'll have to release yer grip of the bar – the green lights have flashed several times now for you to go.'

'Oh right! (Ya cow),' I muttered under my breath, 'I never noticed it, hen, thanks for that.'

I then released my grip, thrusting myself forward and was off like a NASA rocket, but instead of going up, I was going down, and at a very high rate of speed.

Feeling slight discomfort in my back, I decided to arch it. Big mistake! This only acted like engine thrusters on a jet and propelled me even faster out of control down the twisting tube.

One hates to see a big man cry but fuck it, by now I'm screaming like a big lassie, shouting for my mammy as I career out of control, crashing into every part of the flume while hurtling towards earth faster than the speed of light.

Then, '*THUD*!' Oo-ya bastard!

'Houston, he has crash landed!'

I finally came to an abrupt halt in a pool of very hard water about a metre in depth and resembling a big concrete wall.

As I tried to stand up, with my legs now situated at the back of my head in some Praying Mantis yoga position, I'm swallowing uncontrollably in an effort to try and return both my testicles to the small scrotum pocket from whence they came.

Scott and his little *Omen*-ette disciples are screaming and yelling ecstatically with excitement that I have set a new record for the fastest time and some masochistic pool attendant on the other side is shouting at me, 'Ho, big man, stop farting about there and get out that pool before you get hurt!'

'*Before* I get hurt?' I growled back at him. 'You bastard! You might have stopped me at the top of the stairs, before I subjected myself to some unwanted colonic irrigation, coupled with the equivalent of a D and C on a woman!'

However!

Looking back at my day out at the Time Capsule, my totally unexpected speed record did make my son Scott's Birthday and after several short weeks of therapy I did eventually learn to walk again without the aid of a Zimmer. The only reminders left are my high pitch voice and my three Adam's apples!

Plastic People

. . .

I attended a call at a large, popular shopping store in the city centre regarding the detention of a female for shoplifting.

I was surprised to find that the shoplifter was an attractive, middle aged, well-dressed woman who appeared affluent.

As I spoke with her, noting her name, address, etc, she let herself down because she may have given the impression of being wealthy and sophisticated but when she opened her mouth to speak she was as hard as nails, using slang words that even I had still to learn.

She also possessed a good sense of humour as, oblivious to her present predicament, she joked with me.

After speaking with her for a short time I was to learn that she was a professional shoplifter who was very rarely suspected by the store detectives, with her sophisticated upper class appearance and amazing good looks.

Until, she opened her big mouth to talk that is!

She stole to finance her trips to the best cosmetic plastic surgeons and afford their exorbitant costs to change your appearance.

'Ah've hud everythin' lifted up, streetcht and re-located, Ah've hud three breast enlargements, a brow lift, a nose job, my ears pinned back, a tummy tuck, my eyes done twice, a J-Lo bum, a designer vagina, two lots o' botox injections to my lips, anus bleaching, hair extensions—'

I interrupted her in full flow as she rattled off her full medical history and said, 'Frigging hell, Stella! Ye must have been a right ugly wean!'

And Justice For All

· · ·

At a particular murder trial held at the High Court in Edinburgh, where the accused male had allegedly killed a female acquaintance whom he apparently met for a one-night stand, the defence for the accused persistently denied any involvement by his client in the crime.

To strengthen their defence case the accused intimated to his agent that he was prepared to give evidence in his quest to convince the jury of his innocence.

Having reluctantly agreed to his request, the defence QC called his client to the witness box.

The oath was administered and, at the finale of the accused's appearance on the stand, the defence agent asked his client the most pertinent and obvious of questions.

'Finally, Mr Brown, did you murder Irene Tate?'

'No, sir! I swear by almighty God I did not murder Irene Tate!' he replied with total conviction.

After several days of deliberation by the jury, they returned a verdict of not guilty!

Family and friends of the victim were totally distraught – they couldn't believe the verdict of the jury.

As for the accused, his defence and relatives it was huge sighs of relief coupled with euphoria as he looked forward to his reunion with them all after months of being remanded in custody prior to and during the two-week trial.

Released at last from the court, via a side-door entrance he was immediately confronted by the press, all seeking a headline story and photograph for the following morning newspaper.

'Do you want a headline?' he smugly asked the assembled press. 'I'll gie ye a headline that you'll never forget!' he boasted proudly, unable to control his big mouth.

Then, throwing his arms up in the air in a victory salute, he shouted out boldly for everyone to hear, 'I got away with murder!! I beat the system!!'

Members of the public still loitering outside the courts were shocked and disgusted by this blatantly outrageous outburst.

The press photographers and reporters were ecstatic with his unpredictable but sensational response to the verdict.

The following morning the newspapers carried the unbelievable boastful headline, 'I GOT AWAY WITH MURDER!'

However, I can't leave you without giving you a happy ending.

As it was, news of his public confession was relayed to the trial judge, who responded by issuing a warrant for his immediate arrest and subsequent detention.

The accused was quick to point out that he could not be retried on the same murder charge, after being acquitted!

Unfortunately for him, this warrant carried the new and completely different charge of perjury.

During his trial when he agreed to enter the witness box and give evidence for his own defence he took an oath to tell 'the truth and nothing but the truth'!

During the examination by his QC, he stated, 'I swear by almighty God, I did not Murder Irene Tate!'

What a LIAR!

Found guilty of perjury, he was sentenced to fifteen years!

A Night to Remember

• • •

After completing thirty-two years police service, the last twenty-four years served in the Lesmahagow area, PC Duncan Watson knew just about everybody in the village by their first name.

Needless to say, at his organised retiral party just about everyone in the area turned up to honour him and bring him gifts.

At one particular point during the proceedings he was opening up some of his presents together with his wife.

The first one was handed over by the local butcher's twin sons, Gavin and Colin.

Duncan held the parcel up, trying to guess the contents prior to unwrapping it.

'Is it a leg of lamb?' he hazarded.

'Yes,' replied the surprised boys. 'How did you know?'

'Simple boys, I was a polis for thirty-two years!'

Next up was the local grocer's son William, who handed over his gift to PC Watson. Sorry – Mr Watson!

Duncan lifted the large package up and asked, 'Is it a food hamper, William?'

William smiled and replied that it was.

Third one to come forward with a parcel was Tommy Wilson. His family owned the local off-licence in the Main Street.

He handed over his carefully wrapped package.

Once again, Duncan lifted it up and after a brief examination, he asked, 'Is it a case of champagne?'

'No!' replied Tommy.

Duncan examined the package again.

'Is it a case of whisky?'

Again Tommy shook his head and replied, 'No!'

Duncan then noticed fluid leaking out of the corner of the package and licked it, taking his time to savour the taste.

Suddenly, he snapped his fingers.

'I should have guessed. It's a case of white wine isn't it?'

'No, it's not!' replied Tommy, shaking his head. 'It's a Jack Russell puppy!'

No! No! No!

• • •

The worst reply I ever heard in the courts was during a murder trial at the Glasgow High Court.

The arresting officer, a senior detective sergeant with twenty-seven years police service, was called to the witness box and, during his evidence, he was asked if the accused had made any reply to the charge of murder!

'Yes!' he replied, before asking, 'May I refer to my note-book?'

Confirming to the court that the notes were taken at the time, the trial judge permitted him to do so.

He began, 'No, no, no, no, no, no, no, no . . . No, no, no, no, no, no, no, no, no, no . . . No, no, no, no, no, no, no, no . . . No, no, no, no, no, no . . . No, no, no, no, no, no.'

Considering the officer's account of the accused's reply, the judge said, 'Are you telling me that an officer of your experience and police rank noted a reply containing thirty seven noes to a charge as serious as murder?'

'No, m'lord!' replied the detective sergeant. 'It was thirty eight!'

Driven up the Wall

...

Brian Graham was never the picture of health to look at and certainly would not be the ideal choice to represent the police in any recruiting campaign.

He lived with his elderly mother, was in his early forties with thinning hair and had a physical build that resembled an Easter egg on stilts.

After working a single day with him it was easy to see why, because he ate non-stop. Sweets, ice cream, cakes and, most of all, dinners!

We would visit the local hospital canteen during our refreshment break for something to eat and Brian would proceed to go through the card. You name it, he would have it on his plate.

Pork chop, ravioli, bacon, egg, liver and onion, chips, etc.

In order to dispense with the polite preamble, I'm as well telling you outright – he was a fat, lazy, balding, greedy bastard!

Why am I telling you all this? Simply because I caught him out a cracker one night.

On each shift in a division or a traffic department you have your special places to go to for a Chinese meal, an Indian meal, a fish supper and even a cup of coffee, and you stick to them.

What you don't do is hammer someone else's doss or place.

That way, we rule out the possibility of two or three different cops hitting on the same place and abusing their hospitality.

This particular night, Brian and I had enjoyed a Chinese meal from a friend in our area but greedy Brian suggested he felt like a Chic Murray even though he'd just eaten the Chinese!

As it was after our refreshment period I had an urgent statement to submit so Brian was partnered off with big Kenny Morrison.

Out they went on patrol together, Brian at 5' 9" looking like a beach ball on legs and Kenny, some 6' 5", built like a brick shithouse. The ultimate Little and Large!

An hour or so later I had completed my statement and, along with O'Reilly, I was ready to return to my patrol duties.

The supervisors were engaged with reports to check and said for us to take out their supervisory patrol car and give it a run, as it hadn't been used all day.

O'Reilly and I had been out for only a short time when we came across Brian and Kenny's patrol car parked discretely down a side street minus the occupants.

As there was an Indian restaurant nearby I immediately assumed that Brian, the greedy bastard, had decided to have a beef curry chaser so soon after his Chinese meal.

This act of gluttony by Brian, hitting on my friend's restaurant, really annoyed me and I decided he had to be taught a lesson!

I drove around the corner and parked the supervisors' car immediately opposite the front door of the restaurant in full view.

Then we sat and waited for them to come out.

Moments later, the door of the restaurant opened and, as Brian appeared with the carry-out bag containing his meal, he looked out across the road and saw who he thought were the supervisors waiting outside to catch them neglecting their duties.

Quickly, he about-turned on his heels and pushed at big Kenny, bundling him back inside the restaurant door.

The next option available to them was to make a hasty retreat via the kitchen back door, which would lead them to the backcourts where unfortunately there was no proper lighting.

While they pondered this escape route, O'Reilly and I left the patrol car and made our way through the nearby backcourts carrying our powerful hand-held halogen motorway lamps.

We concealed ourselves in the darkness, waiting and watching, when suddenly the rear door of the restaurant opened and the silhouette figures of Brian and Kenny appeared.

They then made their way outside in an effort to return to their parked patrol car, but were confronted with another obstacle.

The entire back yard was surrounded by a six-foot wall.

To big Kenny this was not a problem but for Humpty Dumpty Brian, with his obesity and total lack of any fitness, climbing a stair was a major problem, never mind climbing the wall! Especially in the dark!

Frantically panicking, due to the fear of being caught and disciplined by the supervisors, they approached the wall.

Try as hard as he might, Brian was not going to succeed in scaling this wall without a ladder or a crane and he was not for leaving behind his precious carry-out meal.

As it was, Mr Blobby would have enjoyed more success with the wall.

With no other option available to them short of sticking a pin in his arse and watching him burst and take off –

'*Whhoooosshhh*' – hopefully right over the wall, big Kenny was going to have to give Brian a helping hand.

Kenny bent down to get a good hold of Brian, grabbing hold with one hand of his trouser belt and his other hand under his big fat arse. He groaned as he used all his strength to help Brian up the wall until he was able to pull himself onto the top of it.

Just as he was steadying himself on top preparing for his next big manoeuvre of dropping down into the next backcourt that would lead them to where they had parked their patrol car, I switched on the halogen lamp, pointing it directly at them.

Almost the entire backcourt was illuminated.

Kenny turned around to face the direction of it and froze like a frightened rabbit in our sights.

As for poor old Brian, he received such a fright that, just like the nursery rhyme character Humpty Dumpty whose physical appearance Brian ate to emulate, he lost his balance and, unfortunately for him, he had a great fall, disappearing from our view over the other side of the wall!

Followed, I hasten to add, by a sickening thud!

'All the police horses and all the policemen, couldn't make fatboy slim again!'

As for O'Reilly and I, we also disappeared 'promptly' out of sight, before big Kenny sussed it out who the 'supervisors' were out front and decided to come after us.

Pet Hates

. . .

One of my biggest pet hates is horses, in particular big polis horses.

This goes back to the first time I went along with my motorcycle partner David Scotland, a former Mounted Branch officer, to visit some of his former colleagues at the stables. Cops, not horses!

Standing with David as he spoke with the blacksmith, I was totally engrossed in their conversation when this big bloody horse put its head over the stable door and bit my shoulder, ripping off the epaulette and metal numeral from my red motorcycle jacket.

Not exactly as funny for me as it was for them, and the severe bruise I sustained to my shoulder proved extremely painful.

As it transpired, the following Saturday I was involved in the Orange parade through the streets of Glasgow.

Every motorcycle cop on duty that day was responsible for a chapter of each lodge membership and led them along the designated route aided by a Mounted Branch officer, the support unit in a police transit bus and several uniform beat constables deployed down either side of the parade.

As I led from the front along Tollcross Road, I tried to keep as far as possible in front of my pet hate – the big bloody horse that tried to eat me only a few days earlier!

I stopped for a moment to warn some hangers-on to move back and, as I looked around, the Mounted Branch officer was almost on top of me. That's the Mounted Branch for you!

I quickly accelerated forward to get out of its way and,

as I did, the roar of my motorcycle engine caused it to spook and rear up on to its hind legs.

The rider, unable to bring it under control, just hung on in there as it leapt backwards landing on top of the bonnet of the support unit transit bus, causing excessive damage and stoving in the front end of the vehicle.

It took several moments before the police rider was able to assume full command and bring it back under his control, by which time it had also managed to trample a few of the drunken hangers-on at the side of the march and send several of them sprawling across the footpath to avoid being its next victims.

As for me, I was far enough away from the incident to avoid receiving any blame for what had taken place.

Wembley Weekend

· · ·

One of my great weekend trips away with the police was to the international football matches between the Auld Enemies, Scotland and England.

Every second year, we would pay up our money to the Police Social Club Committee to book your seat on the bus bound for Wembley.

We would all meet up at the Lochinch Police Club in the Pollok Estate beforehand to enjoy several drinks in order to relax us for our long bus trip.

The committee members would then call out your name and hand you an envelope with the excess money you had saved for the trip along with a paper bag containing a half bottle of your favourite tipple and four cans of beer for the journey.

Peter McMillan, our committee leader, would check our names against his list as we each entered the bus.

Within minutes we were off along the Country Park leading to the main road.

Halfway along the road, the cry would go up, 'Ho, Peter! Can ye get the driver tae stop. I'm needing a wee single fish?'

'Could ye no' have gone like everybody else afore we left the clubhouse?'

'I'm sorry, Peter. I've got a wee bit o' a weak bladder.'

Peter went up to the driver, 'Sorry, Don, but can you pull in and let one of the guys off for a pee.'

The driver pulled up and there was a mass exodus, as half the bus got off for the toilet, Peter included.

All aboard, once again, and we're off.

We have only just turned onto the main road, when a shout goes out.

'Ho, darling! Do you and yer wee pal wi' the tartan coat on fancy a trip to Wembley?'

'Cut that out and sit down,' blasted Peter. 'She's just a wee woman out for a walk with her dog!'

'She might be just a dug tae you, by the way, but I've been out wi' uglier lookin' women.'

'Och behave yersel' and sit down on yer seat.'

Peter decides it is time for the big speech and asks the driver to switch on the hand-held microphone.

'Testing! Testing! One, two. One, two. Can everybody hear at the back of the bus?'

A voice calls out, 'Aye – me, Peter! I'll have a beer!'

'I didn't ask if ye wanted a beer! I asked if you could hear!'

'Aw, right! Well, naw, I cannae hear you!' the shout came back.

'Would you try and be serious for a minute until I speak.' He pauses. 'Right! I just want to remind each and everyone of you that you're representing Strathclyde Police. So at all times, I would expect you to be on your best behaviour.

'If anybody needs the toilet, we have a makeshift one at the rear in the shape of two army jerry cans, so make sure you aim right and try not to make a mess. In the event of an accident, there's also a bucket and a mop!

'Now that's all I'm going to say on the matter, so I hope each and every one of you has a good time. Thank you!'

'Right, Peter, now sit on yer arse and give us peace!'

As the bus joins the M74 motorway, they are well on their way.

After several hours of continuous drinking, a voice calls out, 'Has anybody got a spare carrier bag or something? Big Davy is goin' tae be Moby Dick.'

'Him! Goin' tae be sick? I don't think so. He's too fuckin' tight tae part wi' anything!' came back the sarcastic response.

'Here, give him that one|,' I said, handing one over.

Not a moment too soon, as Davy buried his head in it and spewed into the bag.

Unfortunately for him it was burst at the bottom and the contents from his stomach poured all over his trouser legs via the hole.

Emergency procedures were required.

'Cover him up with his own jacket and tell him to lie down and sleep it off, that it will be all right in the morning. Then move as far away from him as possible, so that the bluebottles don't annoy you.'

Several hours later, having crossed the border into England many miles back, Don the driver pulled into a service station for a packet of cigarettes and a short break.

This was also the cue for everybody who was still awake to get off the bus and stretch their legs.

The service station was extremely busy, with football supporters from both sides all on their way to converge on Wembley.

As Clarky and I were walking into the shop, we were confronted by some English supporters,

'Hey, Jock! You don't have any spare diesel on your bus? They've ran out of it in here, and we're almost running on empty!'

I looked at Clarky and he looked at me, then together we said, 'As a matter of fact, we do!' Then Clarky adds, 'We can only give you two jerry cans, but they're full so you'll have plenty to get you there!'

'How much do you want for them?' he asked.

'Twenty quid each,' I said.

'You're on!' replied our new English buddy.

At that point, Clarky and I returned to the bus. I went inside and casually opened the rear emergency exit door and handed the jerry cans out to Clarky.

'Where are you going with them?' asked Don the driver.

'They're full of pish, Don, so we're just going to empty them out!' I replied.

We then humphed them over to our English buddie' and the swap took place for the agreed forty pounds cash.

They were ever so grateful; they even gave us a can of beer each.

Little did they know that they were taking the piss, so to speak!

I can visualise Mel Gibson in *Braveheart* saying, 'You can take our piss, but you'll never take our freedom!'

Quickly, we made our way back onto the bus and within minutes, we are back on the busy motorway, heading for our destination of Epping Forrest Hotel, some forty pounds cash better off and ten gallons of piss lighter!

But most of all, several miles down the road before they realised what they had bought.

However, Clarky felt we sold them it too cheaply.

Somehow, in convincing them that it was really diesel he had also convinced himself they were full of diesel! Daft bugger!

The only problem we faced now, was explaining to Peter the disappearance of the jerry cans when anyone needed to go.

'Oh shit! The jerry cans! We've left them outside the toilets at the service station and forgot to collect them on the way out,' I said convincingly.

'You'll just have to hold it in until the next stop then!'

Time for a bit of shut-eye, to prevent any more questions during the remaining part of our journey.

On arrival at our destination, Peter decided to reiterate his speech of earlier about our behaviour while we were there.

'Now remember, each and everyone of you has the responsibility on your shoulders of representing Strathclyde Police, so don't be the one to let the side down!'

With these few words, we all trooped off the bus into the hotel, where we were allocated our rooms.

Some breakfast and a few beers later, Clarky and I went up to our room to sort out our luggage.

Clarky looked out the bedroom window and said, 'Quick, Harry, check this out!'

As we both looked out across the road, there was Peter, standing outside the pub, holding himself up with a lamp post, being sick onto the road.

I couldn't resist it, and opened the window and shouted across at him, 'Hey, Peter, don't hold back there! Remember you are representing Strathclyde Police!'

Before he could look up and focus where the shout had came from, I had closed the window and curtains.

The following day everyone was up early and all decked-out in their tartan kilts, with me dressed like Les McEwan in my Bay City Roller trousers and shirt. Oh, and a few of them wore the obligatory 'See You Jimmy' red wigs.

How common! I managed to sell mine!

Down at reception waiting for us, were a few ex-pats who had also arrived for the big game, along with a female who turned out to be a cousin of one of our lot.

She introduced herself to us as Ester and there was no

simple peck on the cheek from this burd when introducing herself – it was legs wrapped around you and tongue down the throat stuff.

I instantly dubbed her 'Ester the Molester'!

En route to the Wembley Way we were informed that there was a public transport strike and we would therefore have to walk part of the way.

Walking along the route, we came across the Prince of Wales pub. Mind you, that was not much of a surprise 'cause there was one on almost every street corner. He must be doing really well!

'Let's go in here for a pint!' was the cry, as we all trooped in.

After several beers, followed by some whisky chasers, I made my way to the toilet.

As I stood there, decked-out in my Bay City Roller gear, tartan rosette, tartan beret and the Saltire painted on both cheeks – of my face, I should add – all very colourful, suddenly, the door of the toilet opened and in came this six foot plus, mean-looking black guy wearing a long black leather coat to the floor with lemon-coloured fedora-style hat with a long lemon feather, lemon trousers, a lemon shirt and a pair of lemon coloured shoes.

I thought I had stumbled across Big Bird from *Sesame Street*!

As he stood at the cubicle next to me, looking me up and down, he allowed himself a smile, 'What-choo wearing der, man?' he asked me, as he giggled.

I looked him up and down for a moment, then said, 'What am I wearing? Check yersel' out big man. Ye're done up like a big yellow canary! I suppose ye sing as well?'

He stood looking at me, completely flummoxed by the

accent, as I nonchalantly left him alone in the toilet to try and work it out.

I rejoined the rest of the guys and we left to continue on our merry way to Wembley.

As it was, it wasn't a good day for Scotland.

For a start, the England team showed up and promptly thumped us 5–1. Though in all fairness to Scotland, up until they scored the first goal we were actually drawing with them!

Back at the hotel, the commiseration party was in full swing on our return. The booze was flowing.

Ester the Molester was on the sofa wrapped around two guys like a python probing the ear of one of them with her big horrible tongue.

The lounge area was littered with carry-out pizza, kebabs and fish suppers, as the drink flowed relentlessly.

All the kitchen staff had locked up the fridges and left for the evening, leaving us more or less to fend for ourselves, hence the discarded carry-out meals.

As the evening progressed, the bar-staff were the next to disappear and it was now being run by Peter and Willie from the committee, who seemed at home pulling the pints, as opposed to pulling the burds.

I went upstairs to change and, as I walked into the room, I couldn't help but notice that there was someone sleeping in our beds.

Clarky appeared from the toilet as if nothing was wrong so I said to him, putting my arm around his neck to whisper, 'Jimmy! Someone is sleeping in my bed and I have noticed, someone is sleeping in your bed also. Now I know for a fact it's not me, you or Goldilocks, so gonnae tell me who the fuck it is?'

'So you've noticed, then?' he said, sounding surprised.

'So I've noticed?' I said. 'Stevie Wonder would have spotted them – they're no' exactly invisible. So who is it?'

'It's just big Rab Hagen and his mate. They just needed somewhere to crash out for a couple of hours, but I've told them that afterwards, they'll have to sleep on the floor!'

'The floor, maybe! The corridor, definitely!' I argued.

As it was they both awoke and, after a few moments, they decided to join us downstairs in the bar for a drink.

The party was still in full swing with no obvious sign that it was about to slow down any and we were now joined by the Old Bill, who had their helmets and tunics off and were sitting back enjoying the mood and being offered the odd whisky. In a pint glass!

Ester the Molester had somehow managed to get herself handcuffed to the police sergeant, who thought it was a good laugh – her idea, not his, and her tongue, which appeared to grow like an erection every time she stuck it out, was investigating his tonsils and beyond!

The fun atmosphere amongst our group and the many visitors who had decided to join our party continued long into the night.

Eventually, as the party started to break up, big Wullie Smith and a young probationer cop were performing a taxi service and driving some of the locals home, in the police panda.

Wullie had recently passed his police advanced driving course and was tutoring the young probationer, whilst his sergeant was presently tied up, or should I say 'engaged', with Ester!

Unfortunately, on his return to the hotel the young cop

attempted to take a bend too fast and careered across the road and through a brick wall, before coming to rest in a front garden.

Due to the young man not having a driving licence, big Wullie did the honorable thing.

No, he didn't take the blame, he legged it away back to the hotel along with the young cop!

By now the police sergeant, with the aid of Ester the Molester and a few others, had managed to remove most of his own clothes and was lying half naked and asleep in the lounge area.

His tunic, helmet, epaulettes, shirt, tie, whistle and truncheon were all gone, with only his handcuffs visible because they were still attached to his ankles and the table.

What a job I had fitting his metropolitan helmet into my case!

The following morning, when we went downstairs for breakfast, the bombsite we had left had been cleared. Not a trace of anything!

After breakfast we congregated at the bus in order to load our luggage and head back up the road for Scotland.

While we were standing there waiting, Peter arrived to inform us that Don the driver was missing and he required some help to look for him.

While the search went on, I suggested we load up our luggage into the back area of the bus.

Lo and behold, when I lifted up the door there was Don the driver, lying flat out in a drunken stupor alongside Ester the Molester, wrapped tightly around him like a sleeping bag!

We quickly called off the search, dispensed with the services of Ester and began our long journey home.

With big Wullie driving the bus, due to Don the driver still lying in an unconscious state!

As an epilogue to the weekend, the hotel management sent a letter to the committee saying that Strathclyde Police were 'welcome back anytime', due to their 'impeccable behaviour'!

Roll on the next Wembley trip with the Auld Enemy!

The Tin Man

• • •

While on plain-clothes duty with Stevie Mac, my black colleague, we were to observe some suspicious black Moroccan guys who were making bogus personal calls at some elderly people's houses and cheating them out of their money.

We had been alerted to the fact that the suspects had been seen frequenting a certain shopping area.

During our watch, I saw two black guys coming into the shopping centre and immediately said to Stevie, 'What do you think?'

'No!' replied Stevie, 'They're African!'

A short time later, another black guy entered.

'What about him?' I asked.

'No, Harry!' he said. 'He's a Jamaican!'

Not long after that, another guy appeared.

'Him, Stevie, what about him then?'

'Wrong again, Harry. He's a black American!'

'Him then!'

'Nope! He looks like Puerto Rican.'

I paused for a moment before asking Stevie the obvious, 'Do all you black guys come in a CAN?'

Free Flights Home

• • •

Out on a Saturday night for a social drink with some of the guys on my shift, we ended up going for a Chic Murray at an Indian Restaurant recommended by one of the company.

Once inside and ordering up our preferred choice of meals, one of the guys was chatting away to one of the young waiters who were assisting with our order.

The usual patter, such as, 'Where are you off on holiday this year?' and such like, from our waiter, who gave his name as Tariq.

As it was, Tariq mentioned that he was hoping to save up enough money for flights to go back home and visit his elderly parents, as it had been two years since he had left home.

Tariq proved to be a popular waiter with the guys and, as a result, at the end of the night we all chipped in an extra couple of pounds each for Tariq, in order to help with his holiday fund, to fly home and visit his parents.

Afterwards, having over-indulged and stuffed to the hilt with curry, we all left to go our separate ways.

Next morning, I was within the office, clearing up some paperwork, when I was called in by the duty inspector and instructed to attend a certain address in Glasgow, along with some Special Branch officers and assist them in the apprehension and subsequent deporting of illegal aliens residing within a house at that location, whom the Special Branch had on their list of targets.

We arrived at the large apartment address and immediately gained entry into what turned out to be a converted bedsit with five rooms and eleven Asian tenants who were all present.

After checking their relevant documentation, the branch were able to identify three of the Illegal males on their 'hit list'.

As they were taking them out, I instantly recognised one

of the young men, who had been apprehended, 'Tariq! Is that you there?' I asked.

'Yes, it is me,' came back the reply from the rather dejected young man.

'Don't be disappointed, Tariq,' I said. 'Look on the bright side: you won't need to worry about saving up any more money to pay for your flight home! You'll get home absolutely free!'

Doing the Orange Walk

. . .

Let me give you a wee tip for something to look out for if you are the sort of person who likes to follow the Orange Parade Bond or similar each year.

The older and more experienced officers who accompany this parade treat it like any other demonstration and are professional.

However, this one is accompanied with music from flute bands, a guy at the front performing majorette tricks with a massive big tent pole and usually a big fat guy in the middle battering the living daylights out of a big drum strapped round his neck.

Now if you watch the cops who are involved in the escorting of the parade, it doesn't take you long to spot the new police officers because, within a few minutes of the Bond starting up, the new cops automatically develop an Orange walk swagger.

Arms are swung out to the side and there is definite rhythm as they walk alongside following the marchers, and it's funny to watch the supervisors running around, frantically telling them to straighten up and walk normally.

River City

. . .

I was fortunate enough to be detailed two weeks working with the River Boat Patrol berthed at Clyde Place.

The crew during the holidays consisted of a sergeant, George Ewart, Graeme 'Povie' Edmond and me.

I must admit that it was one of the most relaxing and enjoyable duties I have ever performed, especially with a good crew!

Until this particular day.

One day, we were preparing to sail off when an amateur boxing referee' friend of George's named Eddie appeared at the berth in his civilian clothes accompanied by this pretty young female.

I was slightly surprised as they both boarded the boat and he handed George a bottle of Malt Whisky.

This was obviously their little scam, providing romantic cruises for friends and their burds.

We set off, sailing up the River Clyde, with George standing alongside the young lovers, pointing out the various outstanding landmarks along the way – the Finnieston Crane, etc – when, moments into the sail, I saw what appeared to be a bloated body floating in the water in front of us. I immediately informed Povie, who was quick to confirm it.

I thought I would be told to get the large boat hook and pull it in.

Nope! Nothing was going to prevent us from enjoying a nice wee cruise 'doon the watter' with our guests!

'Tell George "Jean Brody, port side" and then come back!'

I immediately went out and relayed this to George, who

stared at me, raised his eyebrows and turning to the young lovers out on their romantic short cruise said, 'Harry is just reminding me to show you the wonderful views on the starboard side over here, Eddie!' ushering them over to the other side of the boat.

I returned to Povie who was steering the boat towards the bloated body and manoeuvring our way past it on the port side.

'When we get to Langbank we'll pull up at the hotel and you can run up and phone the control room anonymously and tell them you think you saw a body in the water, near to the KGV Bridge. They'll get George Parsonage to row down and pull it out! He must be due another Humane Society award anyway!'

As we sailed through the water George and his passengers were enjoying the views through the bottom of their amber-filled glasses.

Suddenly, our peace was interrupted again, when we received a call from the control room, instructing us to attend a certain location, where the Clyde paddle-steamer *The Waverley* had apparently grounded.

We were to go and uplift the assistant chief constable and a superintendent, who just happened to be passengers on it at the time and had to attend an urgent meeting in Pitt Street Police Headquarters.

With no time to drop off our present passengers, George said to leave all the talking to him, while Eddie's girlfriend disappeared into the toilet, out of the way.

We sailed over to the sand-banked Waverley and uplifted our VIP passengers, who promptly took George to one side and asked him discreetly, who the passengers on board were.

George, without the slightest hesitation replied, 'He's that new councillor who was on the radio criticising the lack of uniform beat policemen on the streets.'

'Oh was he? Well we'll just say hello, then go inside out of his way and leave you to talk to him. I've had enough for one day!'

George then confidently introduced him as, Councillor Edward McIvor, of the Glasgow City Council.

Eddie, nervously stepped forward, shook their hands and said, 'As Roy Scheider once said in the film *Jaws*, I think we're going to need a bigger boat!'

'If you say so, councillor, we won't say no!' responded the ACC, accompanied by some forced laughter.

At that point, George took the ACC to one side and said, 'The council offices contacted us through the traffic office to ask permission for him and his secretary to have a look around the police boat, so I decided to take them out for a sail up through the bridges, when we received the call to uplift you. We were going to drop them off, but he asked to be allowed to come along. I hope you don't mind sir?'

'Not at all, sergeant – it's all good PR. We have to keep them sweet, but if you don't mind, we'll go inside out of his way!'

As they went inside, George looked over at a very nervous Eddie, casually winked his eye and said, 'Are you alright there, Councillor McIvor?'

Eddie just gave a sigh of relief and whispered out the side of his mouth, 'I need a large whisky!'

As they sailed up past Langbank, they received another unwanted call from the control room.

'Could you attend near to the KGV Bridge and assist "G"

Division personnel with the recovery of an unidentified male body in the water there.'

George took control of the radio and replied, 'We are presently engaged with ACC McDougall and . . . '

Just at that, the ACC, overhearing the call said, 'That's okay Sergeant, just take the call. We can get off and you can carry on to it!'

He then 'nodded' his head and said condescendingly to George, 'I'm quite sure Councillor McIvor would appreciate seeing what other duties you have to deal with in your wee boat?'

However, out of their earshot, George called the control room back and asked, 'Could you possibly contact George Parsonage of the Royal Humane Society and ask him to attend to this call?'

Back came the reply, 'Would you please note that we tried to contact Mr Parsonage earlier today regarding this call but he was unavailable to attend. Apparently, he is being honoured by the Royal Humane Society at another awards ceremony for him!'

Not Exactly 'Constable' Ian!

· · ·

Ian McNaughton was a wonderful guy, who never ceased to make me laugh. He also had his own methods of dealing with complaints.

For a short time, we worked together at Rutherglen Police Station.

I remember one particular day when we were working on the Main Street and dealing with the regular complaint of motorists parking across the studs of the pedestrian crossing and causing an obstruction.

On this particular day when we attended there was a car on either side of the crossing committing the offence, so we decided to each take a car and, when the driver of either car returned, we would signal each other to come over and witness the offending driver's details being noted and the 'Caution and Charge' being administered, as well as any subsequent response from the driver.

As we both stood waiting on the busy Main Street I was approached by a woman requesting some advice and directions.

After providing this information, which took only a few moments, I looked up to see Ian walking toward me and the offending car gone.

'Where's the driver of the car?' I enquired.

'She's away! I booked her!' he casually replied.

I was puzzled as to how he could have booked her without a witness. 'Booked her for what? A Tupperware party, a disco, a date?! For what Ian?'

'Parking!' he said. 'I booked her for parking in the crossing!'

'Who did you use as a witness to charge her?' I asked him.

'You! I just told her she was getting booked for parking in the pedestrian crossing and you were my partner and had seen her as well, so she was done!'

I couldn't believe what Ian was telling me.

'What about her driving documents? Did you give her a form to produce them, never mind the fact that I can't identify her?'

'I didn't have too! She said she's going to hand her documents into the office, so I trusted her!' he replied convincingly before adding, 'You'll be able to see her then and identify her!'

With no police corroboration and no note of her relevant driving documentation, this was one driver who was fortunate to have met with Ian McNaughton and witnessed at first hand his methods of dealing with complaints!

Another quick story involving Ian concerned his local pub, Carrigan's, where the landlord just happened to mention he was looking for someone to paint his premises.

'I'll paint it for you!' volunteered Ian. 'Pay me when it's done!'

Delighted with the offer, the landlord left the keys with Ian to do it and left out everything required to do so.

The following Monday, the landlord returned and nothing had been touched.

Later the same day, Ian called into the pub carrying a large parcel under his arm.

'What happened to you?' said the disappointed landlord. 'I thought you were going to paint the pub for me?'

'I did!' replied Ian confidently. 'In fact, I have it right here!'

He then surprised the Landlord by unwrapping his parcel and producing a framed landscape painting of the pub!

Polis Dugs Bite!

. . .

It's a fallacy to think that police dogs can tell the difference between the bad guy who has just mugged an old woman and run off and a good guy who is pursuing him.

Also, the dogs can't differentiate between a police officer wearing a uniform and a plain-clothes police officer wearing denim jeans and a T-shirt.

For this reason, I was always sceptical and extremely wary when any accused person ran off and the Dog Branch were alerted to attend the location and help with the subsequent search.

Best thing to do: stand well back and keep well out of the way, thereby giving the dog and his handler plenty of room!

One occasion that stands out in my mind was when I was involved with three accused, who, after a car chase, crashed the stolen car they were in and ran off.

My female colleague Maureen and I alighted from our police car and pursued them on foot.

After a short distance we were successful in apprehending two of them, but the third ned had gone to ground and was hiding.

A call went out for the Dog Branch to attend and assist in the search of tracking down the missing accused.

Usually, a loud call goes out that there is a police dog in the area – this is warning to the searching cops to move away, and it's also to allow the bad guy the opportunity to come out from his hiding place and surrender before the dog tracks him down and mistakes him for a big juicy meaty bone.

Or should I say, flashes his big teeth and punctures his arse with several large holes!

Lacking in brains, the ned ignored his chance to give up!

Within a short time, the ned is taken into custody – after a short, sharp mauling from Sabre the Alsatian, accompanied by some serious loud screams of agonising pain.

Sabre was rewarded in full, with praise from his handler for a job well done, before being returned to the comfort of his cage within the rear of the police van.

My colleague Maureen also decided to give praise to Sabre and walked over to the police dog van and, with the driver's window open, she put her hand inside and made to ruffle his fur and pat him on the head.

Nice gesture by Maureen, but remember what I said at the start of the story?

As she put her hand in, Sabre, unable to differentiate 'good guy' and 'bad guy', promptly ravaged her friendly hand, resulting in a quick visit to the local hospital for a tetanus injection in her butt and four painful stitches for her wound!

My advice for the future?

Praise the dog handler: they don't bite!

Political Correctness

. . .

'Political Correctness' is fine, but it should always work both ways and not be confined to any one particular colour, creed or nationality.

During my police career, I enjoyed a good working relationship with a black police officer, who also became a good friend.

After several years of working together, he transferred to the support unit and I only saw him during fleeting visits.

On one occasion, he contacted me and informed me he was working in my area and during his shift he would try and call up to see me for a cup of coffee and a chat.

I was busy dealing with police reports at my desk, when the door to the office opened and in walked a uniform sergeant.

As I glanced at his shoulder epaulette number, I instantly recognised he was with the support unit so I said to him, 'You don't have a cop on your shift, as black as two in the morning called Stevie do you?'

He looked at me in amazement and said, 'I'll pretend I didn't hear that remark, but I would strongly suggest that you familiarise yourself with Political Correctness and in particular racial remarks or you could find yourself in some serious trouble!'

As I stood staring at him, pondering my reply, the door suddenly opened and in walked Stevie. On seeing me, he immediately said, 'Harry! How's my favourite white honky?'

'What about that then Sergeant?'

PC – Political Correctness, Police Constable or just Pure Crazy?!

The Parade Square

· · ·

During a parade square inspection at Tulliallan Police College, I was standing at attention in my best uniform, with my creases as sharp as razor blades and my boots polished to perfection and sprayed with Damp Start to give them a perfect shine.

However, it seems I should have used the razor-sharp creases on my uniform to trim my moustache, as along came the drill instructor, Sergeant Blain, on his inspection.

As he arrived in front of me, he stopped and put his head almost into my face and said, 'What's your name?'

'Morris!' I replied confidently, expecting to be complimented on my immaculate uniform.

'Well, Morris, you are a complete disgrace. You are untidy and messy so get yourself off my parade square. Now!' he said.

'With all due respect, Sergeant Blain, I beg to differ!' I replied, in all innocence. 'I spent hours last night pressing my uniform and polishing my boots for today's inspection parade.'

Big mistake! I mean Big! Mistake!

He turned his head away for a moment and said, 'Is that right, Morris?' Before thrusting his face into mine and screaming at me, 'Your moustache is hanging over your top lip like a dead rat! Now get off my parade square and run!'

I then dejectedly but calmly stepped out from my position in the parade and proceeded to walk away toward the college entrance.

I could see the college commandant, with his typical army officer's thick, wayward moustache, standing just inside the crush hall entrance, observing what was taking place on the parade square.

Sergeant Blain, unaware of his presence, then bawled at me to run, but I ignored his rant and continued to walk at my pace, when suddenly I heard loud tackety boot steps coming up quickly behind me.

As I turned around to look, Sergeant Blain came running up to me and screamed in my face, 'I told you to run off my square, Morris! Did you hear me?'

I calmly replied, 'With all due respect, my mother in Glasgow could hear you!'

I then turned away from him and continued to walk, which prompted him to run in front of me again, with his face as red as a beetroot about to explode and his pace stick held like he was about to paste me with it, never mind pace me!

'I'm ordering you to run from my square. Now run!' he bawled out again, becoming more irate by the minute.

I responded by saying to him in all sincerity, 'I think you need to take a Valium, sergeant – you're getting very excited!'

As I walked away from him, he continued screaming abuse at me to run, but I ignored his rants and left the parade square.

On entering the crush hall, the commandant asked me, 'What was that all about?'

Sickened with the treatment I had just endured – considering Patsy McKenna, a policewoman in the row behind, had a much bigger moustache than me – I said, 'He dislikes a moustache, or as he put it, anyone with a "dead rat" resting on their top lip, so I would be wary if you have to perform a parade inspection. He'll order you to run from his square!'

I then scampered off to enjoy a lump of cheddar cheese and seek refuge within my hole in the dormitory skirting board!

Arthur and Paddy

· · ·

One day while out on my police motorcycle, I was dealing with a complaint and issuing parking tickets to vehicles illegally parked.

I was dealing with a small bright yellow VW Beetle when suddenly this garage proprietor, who dealt with American import cars, came running out of his premises shouting, 'Ho, Harry, whit dae ye think ye're daein'?'

I turned around to look at him and said, 'I'm issuing a parking ticket on this car, why?'

He sidled up beside me and whispered out the side of his mouth, 'That's Arthur's!'

'Arthur who?' I enquired.

'Arthur Thomson's! Him and Paddy Meehan are in the old Churchill building. I've been watching it from my office.'

I looked straight at him, while fixing the ticket to the windscreen and said, 'Well, Wullie, when they come out, you can tell them Harry gave them a parking ticket. I'm sure that will really upset they two!'

Then as I mounted my motorbike to leave, I said, 'Better still, Wullie – since you were watching it, why don't you pay it for him?'

Fa-fa-fa-rankie McCoy

• • •

Frankie McCoy was my roommate at Tulliallan Police College during my three months training.

He was a nice guy, but mad as a hatter! I should also add that he was extremely nervous, high as a kite, smoked like a chimney was painfully thin and stuttered uncontrollably!

It was very difficult at the best of times to study for the police exams but with Frankie beside me continually talking in instalments, smoking and fidgeting, I found it impossible!

As a result, I grabbed a blanket from my bed and, with my police notes lodged under my arm, I made my way to the toilets, where I hid away in one of the cubicles to study in complete silence.

After about an hour or so, Frankie worked out where I was hiding and, as I sat on the toilet seat, wrapped in my warm blanket, studying and oblivious to anything on the outside, a bucket of cold water was lobbed over the cubicle door, drenching me.

I then heard uproarious laughter as the culprit ran out and I immediately identified Frankie as the perpetrator.

The same Frankie who occupied the bed next to me and would regularly awaken me at three and four in the morning to enquire if I was sleeping and, now that I was awake, would I like to join him for a cigarette and a chat?

Why me?

How come I got lumbered with a guy who suffered from insomnia and wanted to kill himself prematurely by smoking himself to death?!

Passive smoking had 20 years to run before it would

emerge as a high risk to others, such as yours truly! Cough! Cough! Claim!

Anyhow!

A short time later, still within the cubicle trying to dry my notes off with the tissue paper available, I heard Frankie enter, giggling with laughter.

Stuttering as he spoke, he loudly enquired, 'A-a-are you alright there Ha-ha-harry, or can I g-g-get you a lilo or a waterbed?'

He had returned to get washed and shaved for the morning.

I continued to sit in the cubicle in silence, watching Frankie through a small opening in the door as he washed. Then, just as he was beginning to shave himself, I made my move.

Soaking some toilet tissues, I opened the door and ran over, slapping the soggy paper onto his bare back.

Apart from almost cutting his own throat with the razor, Frankie squealed hysterically in disgust.

'Ya dirty big bastert! Get it off, get it off me!' he shouted, thinking it was the obvious what I had deposited on his back. And I was certainly not going to ease his immediate suspicions in order to make him feel better!

As an added bonus for Frankie, I had inadvertently found a rapid cure for his long-term speech impediment!

And! As an added warning, I later threatened Frankie that if he ever awakened me from my sleep again during the night then next time it would be the Real McCoy I'd use!

What a pleasantly quiet and relaxing two months I enjoyed at the college following that!

Older is Better

• • •

A young probationer police constable was out on his own on foot patrol when he witnessed the following incident.

It appears an elderly, sophisticated-looking woman drove up alongside a row of parked cars on the busy main street in her large Volvo estate motorcar, stopped and waited for one of the motorists to return to their car and vacate a parking space for her.

Moments later, a motorist arrived back from a nearby shop and duly entered his car and drove off, providing a space.

The elderly female was about to reverse her car into it when a young male driver, in a flash sports-type car, appeared from nowhere and promptly drove into the vacant space before her.

The elderly female was extremely perturbed by this disgraceful display of bad manners, having waited patiently for the space.

She got out of her car and proceeded to make the young male driver aware that she had been waiting several minutes for this parking space.

'Too bad, hen!' responded the smug young man. 'It's not my fault I'm much younger and faster!'

Angered by this blatantly disrespectful display, the elderly woman re-entered her car, engaged it in reverse gear and drove it along the entire length of his flash car, causing extensive damage to it.

She then drove forward, stopped her car and, on getting out, she casually called out to the stunned young male, 'You may be younger and faster, but It's not my fault I'm older, with a bigger car and a very good insurance policy!'

Mechanical Touble

· · ·

From *The Adventures of Harry the Polis*

(Harry is working at the front desk of the office, when Orville comes in and slams the car keys down onto his desk.)

ORVILLE: I'm not driving that death trap panda; it's totally knackered!

HARRY: Why? What's up?

ORVILLE: What's up? It wouldn't pull a naked Chippendale stripper off yer granny!

HARRY: My wee Granny wouldn't want ye too!

ORVILLE: I better phone the garage and tell them to come over and tow it away.

(Harry walks over to look out the window.)

HARRY: 'By the way, Orville, it's starting to rain quite heavy!

ORVILLE: So what?

HARRY: Well! If they don't have a spare panda you're going to get very wet!

(Orville pauses for a moment, pondering over what Harry has just said. He picks up the panda keys again.)

ORVILLE: Mind you, I've driven a helluva lot worse than that!

A Lesson in Crime Prevention

· · ·

Whilst working for a short time in the Crime Prevention Department, a colleague and I attended a motor vehicle garage that had recently been broken into.

We went through our routine of checking the entry and exit of the housebreakers and working out ways for him to better ensure the security of his premises. After we were finished we were invited into his office to discuss our conclusions over a cup of coffee.

The owner had to pop out to the nearby shop for sugar.

As we sat there awaiting his return, a young spiky-haired male entered the garage and approached us. I immediately identified him as a local junkie – Ryan Watson!

'Hey, boss, are ye interested in buying some CDs, after-shave or a nice wallet? I've even got a wee tool kit!'

At that point, he placed them onto the table in front of me, spreading them out for us to view.

I was sifting through the items when I noticed some credit cards that had obviously gone unnoticed by the junkie.

On seeing the name on them, I instantly recognised the owner.

'Tell me this, son: did you blag this lot out of a 4x4 jeep convertible?'

'Aye, big yin! It wis a dawdle tae get intae,' he boasted proudly.

'Did you do the door locks?' I asked him.

'Naw, big yin, ye're never gonnae believe it. I just unzipped the plastic convertible cover at the back and jumped in. I didnae even need tae burst it,' he said, still unaware of whom he was talking to and high on drugs.

'Where was it parked?' I asked him.

'Doon at the Stockwell car park,' he replied in all innocence.

'Do you know who these credit cards belong to?' I asked.

'Aye! Me! Ah knocked them!' he promptly replied, reaching over to try and take them out of my hand.

'Wrong, son!' I responded. 'They belong to Inspector Richard Arthur of the Crime Prevention Department in Paisley!'

The junkie just stared at me for a moment, then said, 'Whit? Ur you at the wind up? How dae you know that?'

At which point, I couldn't resist replying, 'Elementary, my dear Watson, we both work beside him!'

Within a blink of an eye, he was off, out the door, disappearing in a puff of his own wacky backy!

As my colleague made to pursue him, I suggested he forget it, as we could deal with him later.

A few minutes later, the garage owner returned, none the wiser, carrying a bag of sugar.

'Sorry I took so long. I hope you didn't get bored waiting for me to return?'

'Bored?' I replied. 'Not at all, mate. Not for a minute!'

However, we couldn't wait to return to the office to contact Inspector Arthur and ask him if we could offer our crime prevention services to him!

The Glesca Barber

...

The other day, while over on the other side of the city, I decided to go for a haircut. I parked my car in front of a row of shops and got out to enter a unisex barbershop.

As I entered, a blonde haired woman approached me and said, 'Sorry darling, but can you come back later? I'm just heading off to the dentist. I'm in pure agony wi' the toothache.'

'Yeah, no problem,' I replied and walked back outside.

As I did, I noticed another hairdresser shop, slightly further along from me.

I approached this one and as I got to the door, a young girl put a sign up in the window: 'Closed for Lunch'!

I was about to get back into my car, when a passer-by said, 'If ye're lookin' for a haircut mate, ye're better goin' tae the new lassie doon at this next block o' shops. She's better and cheaper than that robbin' cow in there!'

'Oh right, thanks pal,' I said, delighted with his intervention.

Just as I opened the door of my car, he stopped an old woman out walking her wee dog and said to her,

'I wis just tellin' that guy over there, not to go into that cow's shop for a haircut – he'd be better off goin' doon the road tae that other lassie, she's much cheaper!'

'Oh aye, son,' The woman called over to me. 'Unisex my arse – it's just a sex shop. She'll charge ye a fortune as well!'

With these kind words of advice, I decided to leave my hair long!

Cannae Keep a Secret

• • •

Several years ago, whilst still a member of the motorcycle section there was a top secret order issued concerning the visit of a very important person to the Royal Concert Hall in Glasgow.

This, we were informed was a high risk, vulnerable VIP!

Several lectures on the security arrangements followed, but at no time was the VIP mentioned by name, being referred to only as 'the principal', with not even his/her gender being divulged, such was the hush-hush.

So secretive was the operation that even the exact time and date of the visit was not being revealed.

When asked for more information about our VIP and his visit, we were told that anything else was on a need-to-know basis and all would be revealed nearer the time.

Later the same day, one of the shift members involved in the escort duty, walked into the muster room with the latest issue of the *Evening Times* and opened it up to reveal the main headline, '<u>SALMAN RUSHDIE TO VISIT GLASGOW</u>', followed by the exact details of time, date and even where to obtain tickets for the event!

So here's a message along with some good advise to all you new 'straight out the box' probationer recruits.

If you ever want to know what is going on in advance of a lecture by the shift inspector, buy the latest *Evening Times*!!

Fancy Dress

• • •

A good friend of mine in the CID invited me to a fancy dress party at his house.

Having never been to one before, I decided to go out of my way to find something unusual to wear.

I attended a fancy dress hire shop in the Gorbals area of Glasgow and after some time searching, coupled with trying on various outfits, I plumped for the Dame Margot Fonteyn costume of white tights and a ballerina's tutu.

Very fetching, I thought!

Come the night of the party there I was dressed in my ballet outfit with a raincoat covering it, bright red curly wig and full black beard (I was not for shaving).

Halfway down the road, I looked in my rear view mirror and saw a police vehicle racing up behind me with his blue lights flashing and I was signalled to pull over and stop.

I immediately decided it was a set up and I was determined that, dressed like this, I was not getting out of my car.

The police officer who approached was not known to me and as I rolled down my window, he asked me the usual questions: 'Where are you going?', 'Is this your car?', 'Are you a poof?', etc.

I sat there like a failed transvestite, resembling something out of *The Rocky Horror Show*, dressed in my tutu, red curly wig, black beard and deep red lipstick! And getting slightly annoyed.

Then came the wind-up.

'Can you step out the vehicle, sir?' he asked.

'Not on your life, mate!' I responded immediately.

'I beg your pardon, sir?'

'You heard me, now fuck right off, you've had your

laugh. I take it Donnie set this up and you just happen to have a camera with you to take a photograph?' I blasted back.

'I don't know what you're talking about, sir,' he replied.

'Aye, right!' I said. 'I suppose you're just dressed up for the night as well?'

After a few moments, he couldn't hold out any longer and burst out laughing.

'You're the third one tonight,' he said. 'In fact the cop before you was wearing a royal blue baby's romper suit with a big nappy and a dummy tit and his wife was dressed the same, only in pink!'

'Who was it?' I asked.

'Davie Mackie! And I even got the two of them to get out the car and stand on the footpath, while I asked them questions, before he tippled it was a set up!'

'Well no doubt he's at the party now, telling his mammy on you!'

With these few words I left to join in the best party I have attended in many a year.

However, one guy was dressed in a large rubber condom, from head to toe.

Someone remarked, 'You look like a big dick!'

And he replied, 'Well, it's a change from getting called a wee fanny!'

Co-Co the Clown

...

I was sitting in the front office area of the divisional HQ, noting a statement from a road accident witness, when all of a sudden the door was flung open and in came a male dressed in a colourful clown costume, with white face, red nose and lips and a red curly wig carrying a large red bucket almost filled to the top with coins of all denominations.

'Right, ladies and gentleman, this is a furniture hold-up. Drop yer drawers and empty yer poackets of all coins. It's all for a good cause!' he said as he paraded his bucket in front of everyone's face.

Some of the unsuspecting members of the public sitting in the foyer did as he asked, too embarrassed to refuse, and dropped some loose change into his bucket.

As he arrived at me, he said, 'Right, c'mon big man, wi' a suit like that you must have a right few bob, so let's see ye dig deep!'

I responded by putting my hand into my jacket pocket and producing my police warrant card.

'Is that deep enough, Co-Co?' I said. 'Now let's see you dig deep and show me some form of charity permit and authorisation giving you the right to collect money in an unsealed container!'

I then relieved him of his heavily laden, coin-filled bucket, just in time, before he disappeared out the office door, legging it down the road in his baggy trousers and oversized shoes.

However, disguised as a circus clown, it wasn't long before Co-Co was recognised trying to look inconspicuous, as he made to mingle with the real clowns who roam the streets of Glasgow on a daily basis, and was promptly apprehended by a uniform mobile patrol and returned to the police office, where he was charged with his charity bucket scam.

It was later revealed that he had come up with this novel idea for paying his mortgage when he saw the generosity of the Glasgow public, giving freely for good causes.

This was one crook committing a profit-making crime in broad daylight while wearing a mask and virtually getting away with it!

Don't Do As I Do!
• • •

One time during my traffic service, I was partnered off with this supercilious twat who liked to make it clear that he was the senior cop and the car we were driving was his!

'You drive my car the way I tell you and you drive it safely at all times. I don't like road accidents and I don't want you involving me in one. In other words, "Don't do as I do, do as I say!" If we are going to have an accident in my car, then I'll have it. Understood?'

I nodded my head and said, 'By all means go for it!'

Later the same day, he went out of our designated area on a private errand and told me to remain in the car.

A few moments later, he came running out from the premises and jumped into the car. 'The gaffer is requesting our location!'

He then started up the engine, slammed it into reverse and whipped the steering wheel around while looking backwards and promptly slammed the front wing of the car into a lamp post on the footpath. Ooops!!

Ah well – he did say if we were going to have an accident, then he'd have it. True to his word, he was right!

Run When You're Drunk

· · ·

During the early seventies when we used Morris 1000 vans as police pandas, I was working with Jack Burnett when we arrested a male for suspected drunk driving. I say that jokingly, because our suspect was very drunk and, as a result, we lay him on the rear floor of the police van.

We then had to drive him from the Croftfoot area of Glasgow to the Divisional Headquarters of Craigie Street.

With Jack and I situated in the front of the vehicle, our accused person was alone in the rear of the van, lying on the metal floor with only the spare tyre to sit on in order to prevent him from rolling about the back.

As we drove along the roads leading to the office, we were fortunate to get a clear road without stopping until we reached Allison Street, where we stopped for a red traffic signal.

Suddenly, we heard a loud bang and, as we looked around, our suspect had kicked the rear doors of the van open and was now legging it, albeit not very fast, across Victoria Road, where, unfortunately for him, he was struck by a car being driven by another drunk driver, knocking him clean onto the footpath.

Luckily, he only sustained slight bruising for his injuries and as a result, after procedures, he shared a cell for a short time with the drunk driver who was involved in his road accident.

This was the first case that I had encountered where a suspected drunk driver was more of a danger to himself and other drunk drivers when on foot.

He also experienced pain caused by drunk driving close up!

Telephone Salesmen

• • •

Like most people, I appreciate we all have to work, but telephone salesmen at teatime get right up my nose!

There you are settling down to your evening meal after a hard day's work, when 'Ring-ring! Ring-ring!'

I can't stand a telephone ringing, I just have to get up and answer it. So I put my meal down and guess what?

'Hello there, is that Mr Morris I'm speaking too?' I'm asked.

'Yes!'

'Well I'm delighted to inform you that you have won the second prize in our "Kitchen and Conservatory Competition"!'

Now, I'm thinking to myself, that's amazing, because I know for a fact I didn't enter any bloody competition but I've won a prize.

'Hold it right there, pal,' I said, interrupting him in the middle of his sales pitch. 'What was the first prize?'

'The first prize was a brand new kitchen of your choice, supplied and fitted absolutely free,' he answered.

'But I've just moved into a new house and it has a new kitchen!'

'Ah! But that's the good news, Mr Morris, because you have won the second prize of 50% off a brand new conservatory in white PVC, with the latest technology in double-glazed units, guaranteed to enhance the appearance of your new home as well as providing you with an extra room for half the cost!'

He said it with such enthusiasm, like I needed one right now.

'Who's going to fit it?' I asked.

'Our highly experienced workforce supply and erect the conservatory and even submit plans to the local Planning Department for their approval and permission, all within 28 days of signing an agreement!' he responded, reeling it off like a plan of his own, taken from the brochure sitting in front of him, no doubt.

'That's bloody marvellous!' I said facetiously. 'And you'll build it onto the side of my house for fifty per cent of the total cost?'

'Definitely, Mr Morris. It's a once in a lifetime offer for you. All I require is a few details to start the ball rolling and I can also enter your name into our ten day "Cruise Competition"!'

'A cruise as well? This is my lucky day. Just copy my details off the competition form I must have submitted before?' I said.

'You probably did, but I just need to confirm them again with you,' replied the lying bastard. 'The usual questions like, how long you've owned your home and do you have a mortgage. I'm sure you know the sort of thing?'

'Right!' I said to him. 'Ask away then!'

After about ten minutes of giving him all my false personal details, he decided to run over them once more with me, to check he had everything required, tying me to his legal contract.

'That seems okay, Mr Morris! So, within the next few days, I'll have our company surveyor call and obtain the necessary measurements and the exact location of where you would like your prize conservatory erected . . . '

Then he hesitated for a moment, obviously double-checking my address on his form. 'You did say number fifty Glasgow Road?'

'No! No! Not at all son! I said I'm in number 5A!'

'Tell your surveyor to buzz me – I'm the top floor apartment up the tenement close and he might get a few other orders for conservatories off my neighbours while he's here!'

Suddenly the penny dropped, followed by his telephone handset!

On It's Own, Number Five

...

Whilst out on patrol one night, O'Reilly and I stopped a black hackney taxi for a routine road check.

At this particular time, the taxi was occupied with two women passengers in the rear.

As we checked over the vehicle we discovered three bald tyres and, as a result, we informed the driver that he was being charged and would not be allowed to drive it any further.

Due to having passengers, the driver called up his control and asked them to dispatch another taxi to uplift them and convey them on to their destination.

Within minutes, another taxi arrived to uplift the two women.

Whilst there, we decided to give this taxi a quick examination and, would you believe it, we discovered faulty windscreen wipers and two bald tyres.

Again, we charged the driver and told him to call his control for another taxi to attend and transport the two women, who now occupied his rear seat.

Moments later, a third taxi appeared on the scene and, just like before, the ladies changed taxi while we quickly checked it out.

Lo and behold, more bald tyres, a faulty light and a faulty horn.

'Summon another taxi for your passengers and join the queue behind the others,' I instructed him.

As he radioed into his control, I could overhear the controller broadcasting back, 'Fur fuck's sakes, whit's going on oot there? I'm running out o' frigging motors tae send!'

As we waited the arrival of our next taxi victim, one of

the women asked, 'Ho there officer, are ye gonnae be long here? 'Cause it's the big Snowball tonight at the bingo and it's gonnae be chocka.'

I informed her that we were awaiting another taxi with no defects.

A short time later, a fourth taxi drove up and the two women had the door open and were entering it, before it had a chance to stop properly. I could see immediately that he had a light out at the front of the vehicle and, it turned out, an expired tax disc as well.

So I informed the women that this would also be parking behind the others and another taxi would be called to attend for them.

'Oh come on, big yin! We'll never get a seat in the hall!'

'In the last 30 minutes, my arse has been in the back o' more cars than a Glesca whore's on a busy night,' said the other.

The taxi drivers were also complaining that the street was beginning to resemble an unofficial taxi rank.

Moments later, a fifth taxi arrived and, like the others before him, his taxi was faulty.

As he pulled in behind the others and called for another taxi I overheard the controller reply loudly, 'Tell them tae fuck right off, nae other bugger wants the fare and I've hardly any left. All of a sudden, they've all clocked off.'

As for the two women, desperate to get into the bingo on time, we had to give them a ride in the back of the police car, with our blue lights on to get them there before the start of the Link-Up Snowball.

Getting out of the police car, one of them remarked, 'We just might be lucky tonight Helen. The bingo will be hauf empty, wi' every bugger waiting in the hoose for a taxi tae come!'

Save The Dug!

• • •

Tour of Russia

During my first visit to Moscow, Russia, with my folk band, representing Scotland at the Scottish Music and Culture Festival, we were treated to a day off midway through our busy schedule.

Our Russian concert organiser Ivan was so excited about our appearance in his country that he wanted to show us some of the wonderful sights available to us, such as the Kremlin, Lenin's Tomb, St Basil's Chapel, the War Museum, Ronaldski McDonaldski, Red Square, the Holy City of Sergei Passad, etc.

Now, unfortunately, after ten days there I was still suffering from the effects of having landed in another country and my bowels had still to adapt to the changes in climate, food and the fact I was still familiarising myself with the local alcoholic tipple of forty-five per cent vodka drunk straight from the freezer.

However, for our one day off, he had specially arranged for us to go on a picnic barbecue out in the country, Russian-style.

Now, I must immediately make you aware that this is November/December time and it's Baltic, as in brass-monkey weather, testicles missing and all that!

The temperature is approximately minus twenty-four degrees: freezin' height!

Unfortunately, he would not accept my lame excuse to decline his barbie invitation and I had to go, along with a couple other members of the band whom I managed to convince, arrange, threaten and force to volunteer to join me on the trip – namely Frankie and Hamish!

The Barbecue Trip

We were picked up in an old Lada van at 7 a.m. the following morning, half dressed and half asleep and bundled into the rear of it and whisked away.

'I am going to take you all to a special family picnic area where, at this time of the year, it will be very quiet.'

He then handed me a bottle with clear liquid in it.

'Here, Harry! Your breakfast for today: good Russian vodka from my personal stock to get you in the mood!'

Having witnessed the driving skills of our suicidal, kamikaze van driver, Mikael Schumacski, for a very short distance I gratefully downed a large mouthful, before eagerly passing it on to Frankie and Hamish, for their turn to suffer.

I hoped that it would numb my brain, in the belief that if we crashed I wouldn't know too much about it and it would be painless for me.

The vodka was strong and yet totally tasteless, with about as much appeal, as a glass of paint thinner!

My host then thrust an open tin of minging pickled/smoked herring into my face and said, 'Here, now eat! Every time we drink we must eat!'

He then demonstrated the method adopted, by sticking his big, manky, rotten fingers into the open tin, pulling out some of the contents and stuffing them into his big wide-open gub.

Not forgetting to lick one's fingers completely clean afterwards!

After miles and miles of snow-covered country roads, our Death Race driver pulled over into a slight clearing at the side of the road in order to sample his share of the alcohol.

This was a man who had scruples!

He didn't wish to drink while driving, for the obvious fear . . .

That he'd spill too much!

However, Frankie, Hamish and yours truly suspected something more sinister and thought we had been driven to this secluded spot, to be blindfolded and shot in the back of the head!

Calm down, readers, our Scottish music wasn't that bad! After all, it's a humorous story book!

Stop for a break and a hug!

Anyway, after sampling about half the bottle and smoking the mandatory six or seven fags in ten minutes, Mikael wants to administer the Russian way of greeting me as the leader of the band.

He came forward and threw his arms around me, lifted me off the ground and, in a bear hug, began to squeeze the life out of me.

Now, I'm not feeling too great. I think I'm about to be shot, along with my two friends, my adrenalin is pumping through my veins, there's fear etched across my face and the last thing I need, standing out in the middle of a deserted Siberian wasteland, miles from anywhere and freezing my butt off, is some big, mocket, foul-breathed, muscular Russky trying to squeeze my insides out.

Now this big bastard is wrapped around me like Boris the Spider, so I immediately begin retaliating using all means of survival: I start punching and kicking at him.

I even introduced his hooter to a couple of Glesca kisses.

After several minutes of what was, to me, a fight for my life, as he attempted to squeeze every ounce of breath out of my frail body, I could feel my life draining away. Then I got my big chance, as he released me to swing me around and tie me into his speciality grip, the famous Russian half-pretzel knot.

Suddenly, with newfound strength, I forced him to release his speciality grip and threw him backwards, hitting him off the van.

'You are very strong boy, Harry!' he said, picking himself up from the ground.

'Yeah! Well just remember that in the future before you mess with me!'

On the Road Again

At that, he lifted up his bottle of vodka and handed it to me.

After a few more gulps, we were back in the van and, with him resuming his position in the driver's seat, we were on our way again.

Where to?

I have no idea, but either I was pissed or his driving was genuinely improving with his intake of alcohol.

Hamish and Frankie were very impressed by my wrestling skills and the way I was able to get free from Mikael's speciality grip, the famous Russian half-pretzel knot!

'I thought you were done for, boss. How did you manage to get free of it?' asked Hamish.

'Yeah! Tell us how you did it,' echoed Frankie.

'It was quite simple, guys! When Mikael had me in his famous Russian half-pretzel knot, squeezing every ounce of life out of my body, while, I might add, you pair of shite-bags just watched! I looked up and saw a penis dangling. So, I leaned forward and took one almighty bite at it!

'Crikey! It's amazing the strength you get when you bite your own penis!'

A Short Time Later

And several hundred kilometres along the road.

'When do we get to the picnic site?' I asked Ivan.

'Not long now, Harry. We're making good time. Maybe another hour!' he proudly announced.

I'm convinced it was a combination of the drink and not wanting to witness our crash site that sent me, Frankie and Hamish off to sleep.

It felt like I had barely closed my eyes when I was awakened by my Russian host.

'We are almost here, Harry. It's just along this private road.'

Arrival at Our Destination

As we all sat upright to look out, our driver turned into what can only be described as an old, derelict concentration camp. I couldn't believe it.

They're not going to kill us; they're going to fuckin' lock us up!

'Is this it?' I asked him. 'Is this the picnic area you mentioned?'

'Yes!' he replied, before taking us over to a large

hut where he informed us we could go in and light a fire. 'Once we get warmed up, we will light the barbecue and begin cooking. I have special Russian food for you and, of course!' At that he held up another bottle of paint thinner.

As the three of us sat around the fire trying to thaw out, our hosts were outside seeing to the barbie.

'I wonder what those big warning signs outside say. Maybe it's Russian for "Butlins Holiday Gulag",' I remarked.

'Probably "No Picnics!" or "Danger, Keep Out. Barbecue in Progress!" ' replied Frankie.

'I'm starving,' said Hamish. 'I hope he brought some big steaks for us tae eat!'

'Here, they're coming in with the cooked grub, thank fuck! Anything will do for me, just to get rid of that rotten taste o' vodka from my mouth,' remarked Frankie.

The Grub

'Right guys! Gather round and grab a plate,' said Ivan proudly.

Now, I don't have a great sense of smell but I'm reliably informed by the guys that it wasn't exactly a flat plate you wanted – it was a bowl to be sick in, due to the smell.

It was totally bowfin'!

I may not have been able to smell it but I could not protect my taste buds as I ate a piece of it. It was minging, shaped like a big sausage and stuffed tae the gunnels with who knows what!

I made my excuses to Ivan to spare myself from having

to eat anymore and, knowing of my stomach problems, he accepted my excuse. But as a replacement he handed me another bottle of paint thinner to myself!

As for the other two, he topped up their plates.

'All the more for us, guys,' Ivan said enthusiastically.

I looked over toward Frankie and Hamish, who were beginning to physically wretch at the thought of it.

Concealed Pockets

Frankie then looked at Hamish with surprise, as Hamish's sausages were disappearing rapidly from his plate.

He whispered to Hamish, 'Where's your grub, Hamish?'

Using hand signals, Hamish pointed to the side pockets of his cargo trousers.

Frankie beckoned for him to take some off his plate also and put them away in his pocket, but Hamish just nonchalantly shook his head and said, 'Eat them up, they're good for you.'

Poor old Frankie: he now had to take huge bites of his sausage and swallow it down whole, with the aid of some rotten vodka to help chase it.

I couldn't resist helping the guys out, since they stood by and watched while Boris the Spider tried to squeeze the life out of me.

'Ivan? Any more food left for the boys? They're too embarrassed to ask you, but they're really enjoying it.'

'Yes guys, I have plenty left for you! Here,' he said, as he topped up their plates again.

Once again, Hamish slipped them off his plate into his side pockets one at a time, so as not to arouse our host's suspicion, as Frankie used sign language to try and persuade him into taking some off his plate. Hamish again refused, shaking his head.

Eventually, when he had finished, Frankie's face had taken on all the colours of the rainbow, as Ivan and Boris began clearing up.

A Walk in the Forest

Hamish decided it was time to face the elements outside and discard his unwanted cargo from his cargo trouser pockets.

Making the excuse that he wanted some fresh air, he left the hut.

Several minutes later, having begun discarding his sausages, Hamish attracted some unwelcome guests, who just happened to find the aroma of the sausages the promise of a welcoming delicacy.

Moments later, Hamish went running round the hut, past the window.

I looked across at Frankie; he looked back at me and shrugged his shoulders.

Within minutes, Hamish again appeared, running past the window but this time he mouthed, 'Open the door!'

Totally oblivious to what was going on and working away cleaning up the dishes with Mikael, I said, 'Ivan? What do the warning signs outside say?'

Without lifting his head, he casually said, '"Beware of Dogs!" This area has a lot of very dangerous wild dogs roaming about in packs.'

Open-mouthed, I looked back at Frankie, as Hamish ran past the window once again mouthing, 'Open the door!' tracked by a pack of five or six of these wild dogs.

Frankie nonchalantly shook his head.

For a moment, Ivan looked up and said, 'Ah Hamish, he is a very fit man.'

'Yes he is!' replied Frankie. 'He enjoys nothing better than a good run out after his dinner.'

A Jog in the Park

Hamish again passed by the window. Having ran around the hut several times, he was still being pursued by his admirers.

'Open the fuckin' door!' he shouted out loudly, while burying his hands in his pockets to rid himself of his main attraction, throwing them as far away from himself as possible.

However, Frankie was enjoying extracting his revenge on Hamish for watching him eat all of his sausages.

As Hamish continued to run around, completing more laps than Liz McColgan at the Commonwealth Games. I was unable to allow him to suffer any longer and unlocked the front door just as Hamish appeared to be on his last legs.

As he fell in the door, frozen and totally exhausted, he said, 'Bastards!' 'I could have been killed out there wi' that lot and you just shook yer heid.'

'Gie's a break, Hamish!' replied Frankie sardonically. 'There's more dugs running aboot the streets o' Easterhouse!'

'Maybe so, but they're considered a delicacy up there.'

'Aye they are,' I replied. 'Especially since one of the families found out that they tasted like chicken but without the flu bug – now they're even more in danger!'

Time to Go Home

After polishing off several more vodkas it began to develop some sort of familiar taste. Apart from the obvious one, mind you – I can categorically state that I've never drunk my own urine!

At last it was time to pack up and head back to the luxury of our room in the boarding house, with the broken window and the blowing gale!

After completing several more concerts on the tour, it was time to leave our comrades in Moscow and head for the hills of bonnie Scotland, where stray dugs are an endangered species and wildlife expert David Attenborough has started a national campaign to 'SAVE THE DUG!'

My Appreciation

· · ·

The author would like to thank you for buying this book and hopes that you had as much fun reading it, as he had writing and compiling it.

The author would also like to thank the many police colleagues/characters who made it possible to write about all this but impossible to tell the real truth.

The author would also like to add that most of the names have been changed to protect the guilty and most of the stories have been exaggerated!

The Harry the Polis cartoons were created and written by Harry Morris and illustrated by Derek Seal.

Harry Morris, who appears courtesy of his parents, is available as an after dinner speaker for functions and can be contacted by email at:

harry.morris51@virgin.net.

Or by post:

PO BOX 7031, GLASGOW, G44 3YN. SCOTLAND.